REUNITED BY
A BABY SECRET

REUNITED BY A BABY SECRET

BY

MICHELLE DOUGLAS

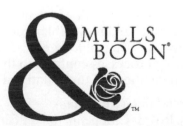

First published in Great Britain 2015
by Mills & Boon, an imprint of Harlequin (UK) Limited,
Large Print edition 2016
Eton House, 18-24 Paradise Road,
Richmond, Surrey, TW9 1SR

© 2015 Harlequin Books S.A.

Special thanks and acknowledgement are given
to Michelle Douglas for her contribution to
The Vineyards of Calanetti series.

ISBN: 978-0-263-26147-9

With thanks to my fellow Romance authors for creating such a strong and supportive community.

I can't begin to tell you how much I appreciate it.

WITHDRAWN

CHAPTER ONE

MARIANNA AMATUCCI STARED at the door of the Grande Plaza Hotel's Executive Suite and swallowed. With her heart pounding in her throat, she backed up to lean against the wall opposite. A glance up and down the corridor confirmed she was alone. Up here at the very top of the hotel all was free from bustle, the very air hushed.

She patted her roiling stomach. *You will behave.* Usually by mid-morning her nausea had eased.

It wasn't morning sickness that had her stomach rebelling, though. It was nerves. She stared at the door opposite and her skin broke out in a cool sheen of perspiration. She twisted her hands together. She had nothing to fear. This was Ryan—blond-haired, blue-eyed, tanned surfer boy Ryan.

An image of his long-limbed beauty and sexy smile rose in her mind and her heart started to flutter in an altogether different fashion. She pressed one hand to her abdomen. *Mia topolino, your papà is utterly lovely.*

She moistened her lips. No, she had nothing to fear. Her news would startle him of course. Heavens, the shock of it still reverberated through her own being. But he'd smile that slow, easy smile, pull her into his arms and tell her it'd all be okay... and she'd believe him. He'd come to see that a child would be a blessing.

Wouldn't he?

The corridor swam. She blinked hard and chafed her arms, the chill of the air-conditioning seeping into her bones. She stared at the door and pressed steepled hands to her mouth? It was just...what on earth was Ryan doing in the *Executive Suite*? She couldn't square that with the man she'd met on a Thai beach two months ago. A man more at home in board shorts and flip-flops and his own naked skin than a swish hotel that catered to Rome's elite.

Stupid girl! What do you really know of this man?

That was Angelo's voice sounding in her head. Not that he'd uttered the words out loud, of course. But she'd read them in his eyes in the same way she'd read the disappointment in Nico's. As usual, her brothers had a point.

What *did* she know of Ryan? She moistened her lips. She knew he made love as if he had all the time in the world. He'd made love to her with such a mixture of passion and tenderness he'd elicited a response from her that had delighted and frightened her simultaneously. She'd *never* forget their lovemaking. The week of their holiday fling had been one of the best weeks of her life, and while they'd made no plans to see each other again—too complicated with her in Italy and him in Australia—but...her head lifted. Maybe this was fate?

Or maybe being pregnant has addled your brain?

And standing here wondering why on earth Ryan was currently ensconced in the Executive Suite wouldn't provide her with an answer. Fortune smiled on men like Ryan—men that oozed easy-going good humour and warmth. The check-in clerk could simply have taken a shine to him and upgraded him, or a friend of a friend might've owed him a favour or...something. There'd be a logical explanation. Standing out here tying herself in knots was crazy, a delaying tactic.

She was no coward!

Marianna pushed away from the wall, wiped her palms down her skirt and straightened her shirt before lifting her hand and finally knocking. A thrill coursed through her. She and Ryan might not have made plans to see each other again, but he'd never been far from her thoughts during the last two months and maybe—

The door opened and Marianna's breath caught and held, suspended between hard pounds of her heart. The haze in front of her eyes slowly dissolved, and in sluggish bewilderment her brain registered that the stranger standing in front of her dressed in a bespoke suit and a crisp cotton business shirt and tie was—

She blinked and peered up at him. 'Ryan?'

He leaned towards her and then frowned. 'Marianna?'

The stranger *was* Ryan! Her pulse jumped as she took in the dark blond hair, the blue-green eyes, and the sensual curve of his lips. Lips that had started to lift, but were suddenly pressed together into a grim straight line.

She stared at that mouth, at the cool light in his eyes. How different he seemed. Her stomach started to churn with a seriousness that forced her to concentrate on her breathing for a moment.

'What are you doing here?'

That was uttered in a voice she barely recognised. She dug her fingernails into her palms. *Smile. Please. Please just smile.*

Her inner pleading did no good. If anything, his

frown deepened. She stared at him, unable to push a word out of a throat that had started to cramp. *Keep breathing. Do not throw up on his feet!*

He glanced away and then back at her, and finally down at his watch. 'I have a meeting shortly.'

A chill chased itself down her spine as her nausea receded. Why would he not smile?

'I wish you'd called.'

She reached out to steady herself against the doorjamb. He was giving her the brush-off?

He lifted his wrist to glance at his watch again. 'I'm sorry, but—'

'I'm pregnant!'

The words blurted out of her with no forethought, without any real volition, and with the force of one of Thailand's summer storms. Her common sense put its head in its hands and wept.

He stilled, every muscle growing hard and rigid, and then his eyes froze to chips of blue ice. 'I see.' He opened the door wider, but the expression on his face told her he'd have rather slammed it in her face. 'You'd better come in.'

She strode into the room with her back ramrod straight. Inside, though, everything trembled. This wasn't how it was supposed to go. She'd meant to broach the subject of her pregnancy gently, not slap him over the head with it.

She stopped in the middle of the enormous living room with its plush sofas and ornate tables and furnishings and pulled in a deep breath. Right. Take two. She touched a hand to her stomach. *Mia topolino, I will fix this.*

Setting her shoulders, she turned to face him, but her words dried on her lips when she met the closed expression on his face. It became suddenly evident that he wasn't going to smile and hug her. She did her best not to wobble. Couldn't he at least take her hand and ask her if she was okay?

Except…why would he smile at her when she stood here glaring at him as if he were the enemy? She closed her eyes and did what she could to collect herself, to find a smile and a quip that would help her unearth the man she'd met two months ago. 'I know this must come as a shock—'

'I take it then that you're claiming the child is mine?'

She took a step back, her poor excuse for a smile dying on her lips, unable to reconcile this cold, hard stranger with the laid-back man she'd met in Thailand. Fear had lived inside her ever since she'd discovered she was pregnant—and she was tired of it. Seizing hold of that fear now, she turned it into anger. 'Of course it's yours! Are you attempting to make some slur on my character?'

She didn't believe in slut-shaming. If *that* was what he was trying to do she'd tear his eyes out.

'Don't be ridiculous!'

Oh, so now she was ridiculous, was she? She could feel her eyes narrowing and her fingers curving into claws. 'I'm just over two months pregnant. Two months ago I was—'

'On a beach in Thailand!' He whirled away from her, paced across the room and back again. His pallor made her swallow. He thrust a finger at her, his eyes blazing. 'Pregnancy wasn't part of the plan.'

'There was a plan?' She lifted her hands towards the ceiling and let loose a disbelieving laugh. 'Nobody told me about any plan.'

'Don't be so obtuse!'

Ridiculous? Obtuse? Her hands balled to fists.

'We were supposed to…to just have fun! No strings! Enjoy the moment, live in the moment, before sailing off into the sunset.' He set his legs and stabbed another finger at her. 'That's what we agreed.'

'You think…' Her breath caught. She choked it back. 'You think I planned this?'

If anything the chill in his eyes only intensified.

Her brothers might think her an immature, irresponsible piece of fluff, but it knocked the stuffing out of her to find Ryan did too.

Maybe they're all right.

And maybe they were not! She slammed her hands to her hips. 'Look, I know this has come as a shock and I know it wasn't planned, but the salient fact is that I'm pregnant and you're the biological father of the child I'm carrying.'

Her words seemed to bow him although as far as she could tell not a single one of his muscles moved. She pressed a fist to her mouth before pulling it down and pressing both hands together. She had to think of the baby. What Ryan thought of her didn't matter. 'It…it took me a little while to get my head around it too, but now…'

She trailed off. How could she tell him that she now saw the baby as a blessing—that it had become a source of excitement and delight to her—when he stared at her like that? The tentative excitement rose up through her anew. 'Oh, Ryan!' She took a step towards him. 'Is this news really so dreadful to you?'

'*Yes.*'

The single word left him without hesitation and

she found herself flinching away from him, her hands raised as if to ward him off, grateful her baby was too young to understand its father's words.

Ryan's chest rose and fell too hard and too fast. His face had become an immobile mask, but the pounding at the base of his jaw told her he wasn't as controlled as he might like her to think.

It was all the encouragement she needed. She raced over to him and seized him by the lapels of his expensive suit and shook him. She wanted some reaction that would help her recognise him, some real emotion. 'We're going to have a baby, Ryan! It's not the end of the world. We can work something out.' He stood there like a stone and panic rose up through her. She couldn't do this on her own. 'For heaven's sake.' She battled a sob. 'Say something useful!'

He merely detached her hands and stepped back, releasing her. 'I don't know what you expect from me.'

That was when some stupid fantasy she hadn't even realised she'd harboured came crashing down around her.

You are such an idiot, Marianna.

A breath juddered out of her. 'You really don't want this baby, do you?'

'No.'

'The bathroom?' she whispered.

He pointed and she fled, locking the door behind her before throwing up the crackers she'd managed for breakfast. Flushing the toilet, she lowered the lid and sat down, blotting her face with toilet paper until the heat and flush had subsided. When she was certain her legs would support her again, she stood and rinsed her mouth at the sink.

She stared at her reflection in the mirror. *Screw-up!* The accusation screamed around and around in her mind.

She didn't know that man out there. A week on a beach hadn't given her any insight into his character at all. She'd let her hormones and her romantic notions rule her…as she always did. And now she'd humiliated herself by throwing up in the Executive Suite of the Grande Plaza Hotel. It was all she could do not to scream.

With a superhuman effort, she pushed her shoulders back. She might be impulsive and occasionally headstrong, she might be having trouble reining in her emotions at the moment, but the one thing she could do was save face. Her baby deserved far more than that man out there had to give.

She rinsed her mouth one more time, and dried her hands before pinching colour back into her cheeks. With a nod at her reflection, she turned and flung the bathroom door open…and almost careened straight into Ryan standing on the other side, with his hand raised as if to knock.

She might not recognise him, but the familiarity of those lean, strong hands on her shoulders as he steadied her made her ache.

'Are you okay?' His words shot out short and clipped.

She gave a curt nod. He let her go then as if she had some infectious disease he might catch. It took a concerted effort not to snap out, *Pregnancy isn't contagious, you know?*

He stalked back out into the main room and she followed him. 'Can I order something for you? Food, tea…iced water?'

'No, thank you.' All she wanted to do now was get out of here. The sooner she left, the better. 'I—'

'The fact that you're here tells me you've decided to go ahead with the pregnancy.'

'That's correct.'

He shoved his hands into his pockets, his lips

pursed. 'Did you consider alternatives like abortion or adoption?'

She had, so it made no sense why anger should rattle through her with so much force she started to shake. 'That's the male answer to everything, isn't it? Get rid of it...make the problem go away.'

He spun to her. 'We were *so* careful!'

They had been. They'd not had unprotected sex once. Her pill prescription had run out a month before she was due to return to Italy, though, and she'd decided to wait until she'd got home before renewing it. They'd used condoms, but condoms, obviously, weren't infallible.

Her heart burned, but she ignored it and straightened. Not that her five feet two inches made any impact when compared to Ryan's lean, broad six feet. 'I made a mistake coming here. I thought...'

What had she thought?

Anger suddenly bubbled back up through her. 'What's this all about?' She gestured to his suit and tie, his Italian leather shoes, angry with him for his stupid clothes and herself for her overall general stupidity. 'I thought you were...'

His lips twisted into the mockery of a smile. 'You thought me a beach bum.'

She'd thought him a wanderer who went wherever whim and the wind blew him. She'd envied him that. 'You had many opportunities to correct my assumption.'

He dragged a hand down his face. 'That week in Thailand...' He shook his head, pulling his hand away. 'It was an aberration.'

'Aberration?' She started to shake with even more force. 'As I said, I made a mistake in coming here.'

'Why didn't you ring?'

She tossed her head and glared. 'I did. A couple of days ago. I hung up before I could be put through...*to the Executive Suite.* It didn't seem the kind of news one should give over the phone.' It obviously wasn't the kind of news she should've shared with him at all. This trip had been an entirely wasted effort. *I'm sorry,* topolino. She lifted her chin. 'I thought you would like to know that I was pregnant. I thought telling you was the right thing to do. I can see, though, that a child is the last thing you want.'

'And you do?'

His incredulity didn't sting. The answer still surprised her as much as it did him. She moved to cover her stomach with her hand. His gaze tracked the movement. 'Ryan, let's forget we ever had this conversation. Forget I ever came here. In fact, forget that you ever spent a week on a beach with me.' *Aberration that it was!*

She turned to leave. She'd go home to Monte Calanetti and she'd build a wonderful life for herself and her child and it'd be fine. Just…fine.

'I don't know what you want from me!'

His words sounded like a cry from the heart. She paused with her hand outstretched for the door, but when she turned his coldness and impassivity hit her like a slap in the face. The room swam. She blinked hard. 'Now? Nothing.'

He planted his feet. 'What were you *hoping* for?'

She'd swung away from him and her hand rested on the cold metal of the door handle. 'I wanted you to hug me and tell me we'd sort something out.' What a wild fantasy that now seemed. She turned and fixed him with a glare. 'But I'd have settled for you taking my hand and asking me if I was all right. That all seems a bit stupid now, doesn't it?'

Anger suddenly screamed up through her, scalding her throat and her tongue. 'Now I don't even think you're any kind of proper person! What I want from you *now* is to forget you ever knew me. Forget all of it!' *Aberration?* Of all the—

'You think I can do that? You think it's just that easy?'

'Oh, I think *you'll* find it incredibly easy!'

She seized the vase on the table by the door and hurled it at him with all of her might. The last thing she saw before she slammed out of the room was the shock on his face as he ducked.

Ryan stared at the broken vase and the scattered flowers, and then at the now-closed door. *Whoa!* Had that crazy spitfire been the sweet and carefree Marianna? The girl who'd featured in his dreams for the last two months? The girl who'd shown up on the beach in Thailand and had blown him away with her laughter and sensuality?

No way!

He bent to retrieve the flowers and broken pieces of the vase. *Pregnant?* He tossed the debris into the waste-paper basket and stumbled across to the sofa. *Pregnant?* He dropped his head to his hands as wave after wave of shock rolled over him.

In the next moment he leapt up and paced the room in an attempt to control the fury coursing through him. She couldn't be! A child did not figure in his future.

Ever.

Him a father? The very idea was laughable. Not to mention an utter disaster. No, no, this couldn't be happening to him. He rested his hands on his knees and breathed in deeply until the panic unclamped his chest.

You can walk away.

He lurched back to the sofa. What kind of man would that make him?

A wise one?

He slumped, head in hands. What on earth could he offer a child? Given his background...

Money?

He straightened, recalling Marianna's shock at finding him ensconced in the Executive Suite wearing a suit and tie. A groan rose up through him, but he ground it back. He'd played out a fantasy that week on the beach. He'd played at being the kind of man he could never be in the real world.

One thing was sure. Marianna hadn't deliberately got pregnant in an attempt to go after his money. She hadn't known he had any!

Did she, though? Have money? Enough to support a baby?

Why hadn't he thought to check?

He passed a hand across his eyes. When he'd opened the door to find her standing on the other side, his heart had leapt with such force it had scared him witless. He'd retreated behind a veneer of professional remoteness, unsure how to handle the emotions pummelling him. He had no room for those kinds of emotions in his life. It was why he'd made sure they'd said their final farewells in Thailand. But...

Pregnant?

Think! He pressed his fingers to his forehead. She'd mentioned that her family owned a vineyard in Tuscany. It didn't mean she herself would have a lot of spare cash to splash out on a baby, though, did it?

He strode to the window that overlooked the gardens and rooftops of Rome with the dome of Saint Peter's Basilica in the distance, but he didn't notice the grandeur of the view. His hand balled to a fist. Had he really asked her if the baby was his? No wonder she'd lost her temper. It had been an inexcusable thing to say.

I'm pregnant.

She'd blurted it out with such brutal austerity. It had taken everything inside him to stay where he was rather than to turn and run. He'd wanted to do anything to make her words not be true. Who'd have thought such cowardice ran through his veins? It shouldn't be a surprise, though, considering whose genes he carried.

He dragged a hand down his face. When she'd stood there staring at him with big, wounded eyes, he'd had to fight the urge to drag her into his arms and promise her the world. That wasn't the answer. It wouldn't work. And he'd hurt her enough as it was.

He let loose a sudden litany of curses. He should've taken her hand and asked her how she was, though. He should've hugged her and offered her a measure of comfort. Shame hit him.

Now I don't even think you're any kind of proper person.

He didn't blame her. She might even have a point. He seized the room phone and punched in the number for Reception. 'Do you have a guest by the name of Marianna Amatucci staying here at the moment?'

'I'm sorry, Signor White, but no.'

Damn! With a curt thank-you, Ryan hung up. He flung open the door and started down the hallway, but his feet slowed before he reached the elevator. What did he think he was going to do? Walk the streets of Rome looking for Marianna? She'd be

long gone. And if by some miracle he did catch up
with her, what would he say?

He slammed back into his room to pace. With a
start, he glanced at his watch. Damn it all to hell!
Seizing his mobile, he ordered his PA to cancel his
meetings for the rest of the morning.

He shook off his suit jacket, loosened his tie,
feeling suffocated by the layers of clothing. His
mind whirled, but one thought detached itself and
slammed into him, making him flinch. *You're
going to become a father.* He didn't want to become a father!

Too bad. Too late. The deed has been done.

He stilled. Marianna no longer expected his involvement. In fact, she'd told him she wanted him
to forget they'd ever met. And she'd meant it. He
ran a finger beneath his collar, perspiration prick-
ling his scalp, his nape, his top lip. He could walk
away.

Better still he could give her money, lots of
money, and just…bow out.

His grandmother's face suddenly rose in his
mind. It made his shoulders sag. She'd saved
him—from his parents and from himself—but it
hadn't stopped him from letting her down.

He fell onto the sofa. Why think of her now?

He'd tried to make it up to her—had pulled himself back from the brink of delinquency. He'd buckled down and made something of himself. He glanced around at the opulence of the hotel room and knew he'd almost succeeded on that head. If he walked away now from Marianna and his child, though, instinct told him he'd be letting his grandmother down in a way he could never make up.

He'd vowed never to do that again.

You vowed to never have children...a family.

What kind of life would this child of his and Marianna's have? He moistened his lips. Would it be loved? Would it feel secure? Or...

Or would it always feel like an outsider? When parenthood became too much for Marianna would this child be shunted to one side and—?

No! He shot to his feet, shaking from the force of emotions he didn't understand. He would not let that happen. He didn't want to be a father, but he had a duty to this child. He would not abandon it to a life of careless neglect. He would not allow it to be overlooked, pushed to one side and ignored.

He swallowed, his heart pounding. He didn't have a clue about how to be a father—he didn't know the first thing about parenting, but... He knew what it was like to be a child and unwanted.

He remembered his parents separating. He remembered them remarrying new partners, embracing their new families. He remembered there being no place for him in that new order. He hadn't fitted in and they'd resented this flaw in their otherwise perfect new lives. His lips twisted. His distrust and suspicion, his wariness and hostility, had been a constant reminder of the mistake their first marriage had been. They'd moved on, and it had been easier to leave him behind. *That* was his experience of family.

He would not let it be his child's.

He might not know what made a good father, but he knew what made a miserable childhood. No child of his was going to suffer that fate.

He slammed his hands to his hips. Right. He glanced at his watch and then rang his PA. 'I'd like you to organise a car for me. I'm going to Monte Calanetti tomorrow. I'll continue working remotely while I'm there so offer my clients new appointments via telephone conferencing or reschedule.'

'Yes, sir, would you like me to organise that for this afternoon's appointment as well?'

'No. I'll be meeting with Signor Conti as planned.' This afternoon he worked. He wasn't letting Marianna's bombshell prevent him from sealing the biggest deal of his career. He'd worked too hard to let the Conti contract slip from his fingers now. Clinching this deal would launch him into the stratosphere.

Conti Industries, one of Italy's leading car-parts manufacturers, were transitioning their company's IT presence to cloud computing. It meant they'd be able to access all points in their production chain from a single system. Every car-part manufacturing company in the world was watching, assessing, waiting to see if Conti Industries could make the transition smoothly. Which meant every car-part manufacturing company in the world had their eyes on him. If he pulled this off, then he could handpick all future assignments, and name whatever price he wanted. His name would be synonymous with success.

Finally he'd prove that his grandmother's faith in him hadn't been misplaced.

In the meantime… He fired up his laptop and searched for the village of Monte Calanetti.

CHAPTER TWO

RYAN GLANCED DOWN at the address he'd scrawled on the back of a Grande Plaza envelope and then at the driveway in front of him, stretching through an avenue of grapevines to a series of buildings in the distance. A signpost proudly proclaimed Vigneto Calanetti—the Amatucci vineyard. This was the place.

With a tightening of his lips, he eased the car forward, glancing from left to right as he made his way down the avenue. Grapevines stretched in every direction, up and down hillsides in neat ordered rows. They glowed green and golden in the spring sunshine and Ryan lowered the windows of the car to breathe in the fragrant air. The warm scents and even warmer breeze tormented him with a holiday indolence he had no hope of assuming.

Pulling the car to a halt at the end of the drive-way, he stared. This was Marianna's home? Her heritage? All about him vines grew with ordered vigour. The outbuildings were all in good repair and the spick and span grounds gave off an air of quiet affluence. He turned his gaze to the villa with its welcoming charm and some of the tension drained from him.

Good. He pushed out of the car. He'd never doubted Marianna's assertion that she could stand on her own two feet, but to have all of this behind her would make things that much easier for her.

And he wanted things to be as easy for her as they could be.

A nearby worker saluted him and asked if he was wishing to sample the wines. Ryan cast a longing look at the cellar building, but shook his head. 'Can you tell me where I might find Signorina Amatucci? Marianna Amatucci,' he added. She'd mentioned brothers, but for all he knew she might have sisters too.

The worker pointed towards the long, low-slung villa.

He nodded. *'Grazie.'* Every muscle tensed as he strode towards it. He had to make Marianna see sense. He had to convince her not to banish him from their child's life.

Once he reached the shade of the veranda, Ryan saw that the large wooden front door stood open as if to welcome all comers. He stared down the cool shade of the hallway and crossed his fingers, and then reached up and pulled the bell.

A few moments later a tall lean figure appeared. He walked down the hallway with the easy saunter of someone who belonged there. 'Can I help you?'

Ryan pulled himself up to his full height. 'I'm here to see Marianna Amatucci.'

The suntanned face darkened, the relaxed easiness disappearing in an instant. 'You're the swine who got her pregnant!'

He'd already deduced from the hair—dark, and wavy like Marianna's—that this must be one of her brothers. A protective brother too. More tension eased out of Ryan's shoulders. Marianna should be surrounded by people who'd love and support her.

A moment later he swallowed. Protective was all well and good, but this guy was also angry and aggressive.

The two men sized each other up. The other man was a couple of inches taller than Ryan and he looked strong, but Ryan didn't doubt his ability to hold his own against him if push came to shove.

Fighting would be far from sensible.

He knew that but, recalling the way Marianna had thrown the vase at him yesterday, her brother might have the same hot temper. It wouldn't hurt to remain on his guard. He planted his hands on his hips and stood his ground.

'So…you have nothing to say?' the other man mocked.

'I have plenty to say…to Marianna.'

The brother bared his teeth. 'You don't deny it, then?'

'I deny nothing. All you need to know is that I'm here to see Marianna.'

'Do you have an appointment?'

He debated the merits of lying, but decided against it. 'No.'

'What if she doesn't want to see you?'

'What if she does?'

'I—'

'And if she doesn't want to see me, then I want to hear it from her.' He shoved his shoulders back and glared. 'I mean to see her, one way or another. Don't you think it would be best for that to happen here under your roof?'

The other man stared at him hard. Ryan stared right back, refusing to let his gaze drop. The brother swore in Italian. Ryan was glad his own Italian wasn't fluent enough for him to translate it. With a grim expression, he gestured for Ryan to follow him, leading him to a room at the back of the house that was full of rugs and sofas—a warm, charming, lived-in room. Light spilled in from three sets of French doors that stood open to a paved terrace sporting an assortment of cast-iron outdoor furniture and a riot of colour from potted plants.

Home. The word hit Ryan in the centre of his chest. This place was a home. He hadn't had that sense from any place since the day his grandmother had died. His lungs started to cramp. He didn't belong here.

Another man strode through one of the French doors. 'Nico, I—' He pulled up short when he saw Ryan.

Brilliant. Brother number two.

Brother number one—evidently called Nico—jerked a thumb at Ryan. 'This is Paulo.'

He glanced from one to the other. Marianna had told them his name was Paulo?

The second brother started towards him, anger rolling off him in great waves. Brilliant. This one was even taller than the first. Ryan set himself. He could hold his own against one, but not the two of them. He readied himself for a blow—he refused to throw the first punch—but at the last moment

Nico moved between them, his hand on his brother's chest halting him.

Ryan let out a breath and then nodded. 'No. This is good.'

'Good?' brother number two spat out, his face turning almost purple.

'That Marianna has brothers who look out for her.'

The anger in the dark eyes that surveyed him turned from outright hostility to a simmering tension. 'You made her cry, you...' A rash of what Ryan guessed must be Italian insults followed. Brother number two flung out his arm, strode away, and then swung back to stab a finger at him. 'She returned here yesterday, locked herself in her room and cried. That is your fault!'

Ryan's shoulders slumped. He rubbed a hand across his chest. 'Yesterday...it was...it didn't go so well and she—' He pushed his shoulders back. 'I'm here to make it right.'

'What do you mean to do?' Nico asked. His voice had become measured but not for a second did Ryan mistake it for a softening.

'I mean to do whatever Marianna wants me to do.' Within reason, but he didn't add that caveat out loud.

Brother number two thrust out his jaw. 'But are you going to do what she *needs* you to do?'

He thrust his jaw out too. 'I will not *force* her to do anything. I refuse to believe I know better than she does about what she needs. She's a grown woman who knows her own mind.'

The brothers laughed—harsh, scornful laughter as if he had no idea what he was talking about.

Ryan's every muscle tensed and he could feel his eyes narrow to slits as a dangerous and alien recklessness seized him. 'Have the two of you been bullying her or pressuring her in any way?'

Had they been pressuring her to keep the baby due to some outdated form of conservatism? Or... Had they been pressuring her to give the baby up because of scandal and—?

'And what if we have, Paulo?' brother number two mocked. 'What then?'

'Then I will beat the crap out of you!'

It was stupid, reckless, juvenile, but he couldn't help it. Marianna was pregnant! She needed calm and peace. She needed to take care of her health. She didn't need to be worried into an early grave by two overprotective brothers.

The brothers stared at him. Neither smiled but their chins lowered. Nico pursed his lips. The other rolled his shoulders. Ryan stabbed a finger first at brother number one and then at brother number two. 'Let me make one thing crystal clear. *I am not abandoning my child.* Marianna and I have a lot we need to sort out and we're going to do it without interference from either one of you.'

Raised voices drifted out across the terrace as Marianna marched towards the villa. She rolled her eyes. What on earth were Angelo and Nico bickering about now? She stepped into the room…

And froze.

Ryan!

A shock of sweet delight pierced through the numbness she'd been carrying around with her all day, making her tingle all over.

No! She shook it off. She would *not* be delighted to see him. Of all the low-down—

His gaze speared to her and the insults lining up in her mind dissolved.

'Hello, Marianna.' His voice washed over her like warm, spiced mead and she couldn't utter a single sound. She dragged her gaze away to glance at her brothers. Angelo raised a derisive eyebrow. 'Look what the cat dragged in, Marianna.' He folded his arms. 'Paulo.'

Ryan ignored his mockery to stride across to her. He took her hand in his and lifted it to his lips. Her heart fluttered like a wild crazy thing. 'Are you okay?' He uttered the words gently, his eyes as warm as the morning sun on a Thai beach.

While it wasn't a hug and an 'it'll all be okay' there was no mistaking the sincerity of his effort. She hadn't expected to see him again. Ever. She'd thought he'd have run for the hills.

'Marianna?'

She loved the way he said her name. It made things inside her tight and warm and loose and aching all at once. His grip on her hand tightened and she shook herself. 'Yes, thank you.' But the sudden sexual need that gripped had her reefing her hand from his. They were no longer Ryan and Mari, free and easy holidaymakers. They were Ryan and Marianna, prospective parents. That put a very different spin on matters and the sooner she got her head around that, the better.

This wasn't about him and her. It was about him and the baby. Did he want to be involved with the baby? If he did, and if he was sincere, then they would have to sort something out…come to some kind of arrangement.

Shadows gathered in Ryan's eyes. She swallowed, recalling the way she'd thrown the vase at him. 'And you? Are you okay?'

She watched him as he let out a slow breath. 'As you haven't thrown anything at me yet, then yes—so far, so good.'

Behind him, Nico groaned. 'You threw something at him?' he said in Italian.

'He made me angry,' she returned in her native tongue, trying not to wince at how rash and impetuous it must make her sound.

With a sigh she glanced back at Ryan. 'Have you been formally introduced to my brothers?'

'I've not had that pleasure, no.'

His tone told her they'd been giving him a hard time, but he didn't seem too fazed by it. A man who could hold his own against her two overprotective brothers? Maybe there were hidden depths to Ryan she had yet to plumb. *Let's hope so,* mia topolino. She wanted her baby to have a father who would love it.

She couldn't get her hopes up on that head, though. She recalled all the things he'd said yesterday and her stomach started to churn. He might just be here to offer her some kind of financial arrangement—to buy her off.

Keep your cool until you know for sure.

She tossed her head. She meant to keep her cool regardless.

She pulled herself back to the here and now and gestured. 'This is my oldest brother, Angelo, and this is Nico. He manages our vineyard.' She couldn't keep a thread of pride from her voice. She adored both of her brothers. 'And this—' she went to touch Ryan's arm and then thought the better of it '—is Ryan White.'

The men didn't shake hands.

Angelo gave a mock salute. 'Paulo.'

Ryan glanced down at her with a frown in his eyes. She waved a dismissive hand through the air. 'It is a stupid joke of theirs. Don't pay them any mind.'

'Marianna's boyfriends don't last too long,' Nico said. A deliberate jab, no doubt, at what he saw as her flightiness. 'Angelo and I decided long ago it was pointless remembering names.'

Angelo folded his arms. 'How long do you think this one will last, Nico?'

'Six weeks.'

'I'll give him four. He doesn't look as if he has what it takes to keep Mari's interest.'

'True. I can't see that he has anything more to offer her than any of the others.'

A clash of gazes ensued between the men and in some dark, dishonourable place in her heart the silent interchange fascinated her.

She tried to shake herself from under its spell. *What is wrong with you?*

With a snort, Ryan turned back to her. 'May I take you out to lunch?'

She glanced at Nico, who told her in Italian to take the afternoon off. 'Give him a chance.'

'You owe it to him, *bella*,' Angelo added.

What on earth…? She pulled in a breath, grateful her brothers spoke in their native tongue. She recalled the raised voices she'd heard when she'd approached the villa. 'How good is your Italian?' she asked Ryan.

'Very poor.' He glanced at Angelo and Nico. 'Which is probably a blessing.'

She folded her arms and glared at her brothers, reverting back to Italian. 'Did you put him up to this?'

Nico shook his head. 'But if this man is the father of your baby, you need to speak with him.'

'I did that yesterday!'

His gaze skewered her. 'Did you? Or did you merely drop your bombshell, throw a temper tantrum and run?'

Her face started to burn. It took an effort of will not to press her hands to her cheeks to cool them. Nico had a point.

Another thought slid into her then and she stared at each man in turn. If Angelo and Nico saw her dealing with the father of her prospective child maturely and responsibly, then that would help them see her as a responsible adult who could be trusted to make sensible decisions about her life, right? Not to mention the life of her unborn child. Maybe this was one way she could prove to them that she wasn't a failure or a flake.

She glanced down at her hands. Ryan *was* the father of her child. If he wanted to be a part of their baby's life…

Lifting her chin, she turned back to Ryan and reverted to English. 'I need to talk to Nico about the vines for a few minutes and then we can go for lunch.'

He nodded and glanced around. 'What if I wait over there?' He pointed to a sofa on the other side of the room.

She pressed her hands together. 'Perfect.' She wasn't so sure how perfect it was when Angelo followed him and took the seat opposite.

'Is there anything wrong with the vines?' Nico said, his face suddenly alive and intent.

'The soil is perfect! You have done an admirable job, Nico.'

'You set the groundwork before you left.'

Did he really believe that? Did he really think her an asset to the vineyard? She shook the thought off. She would prove herself to him. And Angelo. She was good at her job. 'The grapes are maturing as they should, but if the long-range weather forecast is to be believed, then we need to consider irrigating the northern slopes sooner than usual.'

'You mentioned last week something about new irrigation methods you'd picked up in Australia?'

She and Nico moved to the dining table to go over her report, but all the time her mind was occupied with Ryan. She heard him try to make small talk about the vineyard, but Nico asked her a question and she didn't hear Angelo's reply.

The next time she had a chance to glance up it was to see Ryan flicking a business card across to Angelo with the kind of mocking arrogance that would've done both of her brothers proud.

She dragged her attention back to Nico. 'From

what I've seen so far, Nico, the vines are in great shape. I'll continue with my soil samples over the next week and checking the vines for any signs of pests or moulds, but...' she shrugged '...so far, so good. Seems to me we're on track for the fattest, juiciest grapes in the history of winemaking.'

It might've been an exaggeration, but it made her brother smile as it was supposed to. 'I'm glad you're home, Mari.'

Guilt slid in between her ribs at that. She'd been Irresponsible Marianna too long. She'd left Nico to run the vineyard on his own and now... She rubbed a hand across her chest. And now both of her brothers thought her an incompetent—a screw-up—that they needed to look after. They hadn't said as much, of course, but she knew.

'I'm not sure I like him.'

She glanced up to find Nico staring at Ryan.

She'd liked the man she'd met in Thailand. She'd liked him a lot. She hadn't liked the man she'd met at the Grande Plaza Hotel yesterday, though. Not one little bit. The man sitting on the sofa...she wasn't sure she knew *him* at all.

She touched Nico's arm. 'What matters is if I like him or not, I think, Nico.'

The faintest of smiles touched his lips. 'You always like them, Marianna...for a week or two.'

'This one is different.'

'Is he?'

Yes. He was the father of her unborn child.

CHAPTER THREE

'THE FOOD HERE is superb,' Marianna told Ryan, staring at the *arancini* balls the waitress set in front of her. Very carefully she drew the scent into her lungs and then gave up a silent thanks when her stomach didn't rebel.

It didn't mean she had an appetite, though. When Ryan didn't pick up his cutlery to sample his fettuccine, she figured he wasn't all that hungry either. She leaned back and folded her hands in her lap. 'So…it wasn't food you wanted after all.'

'I wanted to talk to you…privately.'

Daniella, the maître d', had taken one look at Marianna's face and seated them in the most secluded corner of the restaurant. Marianna was glad now that she had. 'Well…talk.'

He picked up his fork and tested each tine with his index finger. He made as if to stab at a mushroom, but he set the fork down again and shuffled back in his seat. Marianna had no interest in making the way easy for him, but his continuing silence started to stretch her nerves thin.

'I did an Internet search on you last night.'

His gaze speared to hers.

'I know you're some hotshot consultant who comes in and saves companies who are on the brink of bankruptcy. I know you're worth a lot of money.' She shook her head. Her idea of him being some free and easy gypsy type must've had him laughing up his sleeve. She suspected her hope that he would love their child would prove just as ridiculous. 'So let's clear this up right now. I do not want your money. I have no intention whatsoever of making any claim on it. No doubt you've come prepared with papers you've had your lawyers draw up.'

The darkness in his eyes throbbed between them. Marianna swallowed. 'C'mon, then.' She beckoned with both hands. 'Pull them out and let me sign them. Then, perhaps, we can enjoy our meal before going our separate ways.'

'You think that's why I'm here?'

She arranged her serviette in her lap and then folded her hands on the table. 'Isn't it?'

He reached out as if to take her hand, but pulled back to rub his nape instead. Marianna pulled her hands into her lap and glanced away. Looking at him… It was too hard. It hurt all of the sore places inside her.

'I'm sorry I didn't react well yesterday. Your news blind-sided me. I was…stunned. In shock.'

That was one way of putting it.

'At the time I didn't consider how hard it must've been for you to deal with the news all on your own. I'm sorry.'

His apology surprised her.

She grimaced. She hadn't exactly broached the subject of her pregnancy gently, had she? She'd shot the news at him like a torpedo…and she'd expected him to deal with that with grace? Her brothers would blame it on her flair for the dramatic. The truth of the matter was she'd taken one look at the stranger who'd confronted her yesterday and had panicked.

He had another think coming, though, if he expected her to apologise for that! She seized her cutlery and sliced off a sliver of food, lifting it towards her mouth.

'What I'm trying to say, Marianna, is that I have no intention of abandoning my child.'

She dropped her knife and fork back to her plate, the morsel untouched. Her heart pounded. 'And what if you have no say in that?' He'd said he didn't want a baby. *Ever.* She wasn't letting a man like that anywhere near her child.

He turned grey. 'Please don't prevent me from being a part of my child's life. I know I behaved badly yesterday and I know I'm not what you thought I was, but then you're not what I thought you were either.'

That arrow found its mark.

He leaned towards her, his eyes ablaze. 'I know what it's like to feel unwanted by one's parents.'

Something inside her stilled, and then started to ache at the pain he tried to mask in the depths of his eyes.

'I have no intention of letting a child of mine feel rejected like that.'

Yesterday, before their unfortunate meeting, she'd expected him to be a part of their child's life…regardless of anything else that might or might not happen between them. She passed a hand across her eyes and tried to still the sudden pounding of her heart. 'How do you think this can work?'

He captured her hand and forced her to look at him. The sincerity in his face caught at her. 'Marianna, I will do anything you ask of me. Anything except…' He swallowed.

'Except?'

'Walk away from our child. Or…'

'Or?'

'Marry you.'

She reclaimed her hand and glared. 'Who mentioned anything about marriage?'

'I didn't say I thought that's what you wanted. I—'

'Good! Because I don't! We don't even know each other!' A fact that was becoming increasingly clear. 'What kind of antiquated notions do you think I harbour?'

'Don't fly off the handle.' He glared right back at her. 'I thought it wise to make myself and my intentions clear. Your brothers seem very traditional and—'

'They're protective, not stupid! They wouldn't want me marrying some man just because I'm pregnant. For heaven's sake, women get pregnant all the time—single women. No one expects them to get married any more. No one thinks it's shameful or a scandal.'

He leaned towards her, his eyes intent. 'So your

brothers haven't been pressuring you about the baby?'

'What are you talking about?'

He eyed her warily. 'Don't fly off the handle again.'

Her hands clenched. 'Do *not* tell me what to do.'

His eyes narrowed, turning cold and hard, and Marianna had to suppress a shiver, but she held her ground. He folded his arms and eased back. 'I was concerned your brothers might've been pressuring you to keep the baby when you didn't want to. Or, alternatively, pressuring you to give it away when you wanted to keep it.'

'They've been nothing but supportive.' She'd screwed up, again, but she had their support. They might think her a total write-off, but she would always have their support.

But if they were pressuring her, had Ryan meant to intervene on her behalf? The idea intrigued her.

She moistened her lips. 'What do *you* mean to pressure me to do?'

'It seems to me I have very little say in the matter.' He picked up his fork again, put it down. 'It's your body and your life that will be most immediately impacted. I'll support you in whatever decisions you make. If there's anything practical I can do, I hope you'll let me know.'

He made her feel like a spoilt child.

'Correct me if I'm wrong, but yesterday I was under the impression that you meant to keep the baby.' He frowned, looking not altogether pleased. 'Have you changed your mind?'

She shook her head. An unplanned pregnancy hadn't been part of her life plan, but… She'd always intended to become a mother one day. She'd just thought she'd be married to the man of her dreams first. Still, the moment the pregnancy test had confirmed that she was, indeed, pregnant, she'd been gripped by such a fierce sense of protectiveness for the new life growing inside her that, while she'd considered all of the options available to her, the only one that had made any sense to her *emotionally* was to keep her baby. To love it. To give it a wonderful life. 'I'm going to have this baby and I'm going to raise it and love it.'

He nodded. 'I know I've made it clear that I'm a lone wolf—I never intend to marry—but I do mean to be a father to this child.'

She rubbed her temples, unable to look at him. She finally picked up her cutlery and ate a bite of food.

He honed in on her unease immediately. 'What's wrong with that? Why do you have a problem with that?'

'Lone wolves don't hang around to help raise the young, Ryan. They hotfoot it to pastures greener.' Nothing he said made sense. 'If you intend to never marry, that's your business. But I don't see how you can be both a lone wolf and any kind of decent father.'

She raised her hands, complete with cutlery, heavenwards. 'To be a good father you need to be connected to your child, involved with it. When it needs you to, you have to drop everything at a moment's notice. You have to…' She met his gaze across the table. 'You have to put its needs above your own…even when you're craving solitude and no strings.'

He swallowed.

'A baby is just about the *biggest strings* that you can ever have.' She leaned towards him. 'Ryan, you will be bound to this child for life. Are you prepared for that?'

He'd gone pale. He stared back at her with eyes the colour of a stormy sea.

'For a start, how do you mean to make it work? How…?' She rubbed a hand across her brow. 'I can tell you how I mean to make it work. I mean to stay here in Monte Calanetti where I have a good job, a family I love and a network of friends. My entire network of support is here. What do you mean to do—drop in for a few days here and there every few months when you're between assignments?'

'I...'

She massaged her temples. 'I don't know what your definition of a good father might be, but that's not mine.'

'Mine neither.' Hooded eyes surveyed her. 'You have to realise I've only had a day so far to try and think things through.'

He wanted her to cut him some slack, but...this was her child's life they were talking about.

'I did have a thought during the drive up here,' he said. The slight hesitancy in his voice coupled with the deep, whisky tones made the flutters start up in her stomach.

She swallowed. 'Okay, run it by me, then.'

'What if I buy a house for you and the baby, and whenever I can get back here I can stay and spend time with our child? I do mean to get back here as often as I can.'

He wanted what? She seized her fork and shoved lukewarm *arancini* into her mouth to stop from yelling at him. Yelling wouldn't be mature or adult. It wouldn't help their child. Her grip on her cutlery tightened. Oh, but it would be entirely understandable! Any innocent bystander would surely agree?

'You don't like the idea?'

She shook her head and chewed doggedly.

'But the house would be yours and—'

He broke off when she pushed a whole half of an *arancini* ball into her mouth.

He rubbed a hand across his jaw. 'Okay, what's wrong with that plan?'

It took her a moment of chewing and swallowing and sipping of water before she could trust herself to answer with any equanimity. 'You don't ever mean to marry, no?'

His frown deepened. 'Right.'

'But it doesn't necessarily follow that I won't.'

He gazed at her blankly.

'The mother, her baby, her ex-lover and her husband,' she quipped. 'All under one roof? How cosy. *Not!*' She stabbed her fork at him. '*Not* going to happen.'

He dragged a hand down his face, before glancing back at her with eyes that throbbed.

'Ryan, I will organise my own life—my own house and furniture, not to mention my work. If you want contact with the baby, then that's fine. I have no intention of stopping you—but nor do I have any intention of being your glorified housekeeper while you do it. Buy a house in Monte Calanetti by all means. Feel free to hire a housekeeper and a nanny to help you with housework and the baby, but don't think you're going to cramp my life like that.'

'You mean to marry one day?'

Of all the things she'd just said, *that* was what he wanted to focus on? 'Of course I do.' And while they were on the topic… 'I mean to have more babies too.'

He paled. 'And do you think this future husband of yours will love our child?'

What kind of question was that? How on earth could he think it possible for her to fall in love with someone who wouldn't love her child too?

He sat back, his spine ramrod-rigid. 'My offer of a house wasn't meant to curtail your freedom. I can see now it was ill considered. You're right—it would never work. I'm sorry.'

Did he really want what was best for their baby? She recalled the way his eyes had flashed when he'd said he wouldn't let his child feel unloved or rejected. They were on the same side, but it didn't feel that way.

He pressed his lips together. 'We're going to have to learn to work together on this.'

'Yes.' At least they agreed about that.

He thrust a finger at her. 'And I can tell you now that I won't be foisting my child off onto some nanny.'

That scored him a few brownie points, but... 'What do you know about caring for a baby? Have you ever fed one and then burped it? Have you ever changed a diaper?'

He glanced away.

Marianna choked. 'Please tell me you've at least held one.'

He didn't answer, but his expression told its own story. Why on earth was he here? If he avoided children with the same ferocity he did marriage, why hadn't he run for the hills?

I know what it's like to feel unwanted.

Her heart suddenly burned for the small boy that was still buried deep in the man opposite her. He'd been hurt badly by his childhood, that much was evident, and he wanted to do better by his child. She couldn't help but applaud that.

'Hell, Marianna!' He swung back. 'I know nothing about babies or children. They're a complete mystery to me. But I can learn and I will love our child.'

For their baby's sake, she hoped he was right.

He'd gone so pale it frightened her. 'Can you teach me what I need to know?'

'Me?' The word squeaked out of her.

'There isn't anyone else I can ask.'

The implication of his lone-wolf ways hit her then and she gulped. It occurred to her that he might need this baby more than he realised. She gripped her hands together in her lap. Admittedly, she and he did have to learn to work together—that'd be in the best interests of their child. And seeing the two of them working things out together in a rational, *adult* way would put both Angelo's and Nico's minds at rest.

If Ryan really was willing to make an effort then…then their baby deserved to know him, to have him in its life. Her baby deserved to be loved by as many people as possible. And… She swallowed. And if Ryan did suddenly decide that he couldn't handle fatherhood, it'd be better to discover that now, before the baby was born.

You mean to test him to see if he's worthy?

Was that what she was doing?

Who's going to test you?

She closed her eyes.

'Is everything okay with your meals?'

Marianna's eyes sprang open to find Daniella frowning at their barely touched plates. 'The food is divine,' Marianna assured her.

The maître d' planted her hands on her hips. 'Would you like me to get Raffaele to prepare something else for you?'

'No, no, Daniella. Honestly, the food is wonderful. It's just...' Marianna pulled in a deep breath. 'Well, the fact of the matter is I'm pregnant, and food at the moment—any food—is a bit...iffy.'

Daniella stared, and then an enormous smile spread across her face. 'Marianna! What exciting news! Congratulations!'

She bent and hugged her and Marianna's throat thickened. 'I...thank you.'

The maître d' tapped a finger against her lips and then suddenly winked and wheeled away. Her smile speared straight into Marianna's heart. She swallowed and blinked hard. She stared down into her lap and fiddled with her napkin.

Ryan ducked his head and tried to catch her eye. 'Are you okay?'

'Uh-huh.' She nodded.

He brought a fist up to his mouth. 'Are you crying?'

Marianna lifted her napkin and buried her face in it for a moment, before drawing back and dabbing at her eyes.

Ryan stared at her as if he didn't have a clue what to do. He shuffled on his seat, but he didn't run. 'What's wrong?'

'Nothing's wrong. It's just... Daniella is the first person who's actually congratulated me and...and it was nice. The news of a baby should be celebrated.'

Ryan's face darkened. 'I thought you said your brothers had been supportive.'

'They have been, but...well, the pregnancy was obviously unplanned and...' They hadn't meant to make her feel as if she'd messed up. 'They've been worried about me.'

On the table, his hand clenched. 'And I acted like a damn jerk.'

She blew out a breath. She hadn't really given him much of a chance to act any other way.

Daniella returned with an enormous slice of chocolate cherry cake—Marianna's favourite. 'Compliments of the chef,' she said, setting it down with a flourish.

Darn it! Her throat went all thick again. Her

emotions were see-sawing so much at the moment they were making her dizzy. 'Thank him for me,' she managed.

She promptly curved her spoon through it and brought it to her mouth, closing her eyes in ecstasy as the taste hit her. She opened them again to find Ryan staring at her as if mesmerised. A strange electricity started to hum through her blood.

They both glanced away at the same time.

Her heart pounded. Okay. In her mind she drew the word out. She and Ryan might be virtual strangers—in their real world incarnations—but they still generated heat. A lot of heat. She ate more cake. Ryan set to work on his fettuccine. They studiously avoided meeting each other's eyes.

If they were going to successfully co-parent, they were going to have to ignore that heat.

What a pity.

She choked when the unbidden voice sounded in her head. She was shameless!

'Everything okay?'

She pulled in a breath. 'If we want this to work, Ryan—'

'I for one *really* want it to.'

His vehemence made her feel less alone. She couldn't afford to trust it too deeply, to enjoy it too much, but…it was still kind of nice. 'Then we need to be really, *really* honest with each other, yes?'

He set his knife and fork down. 'Yes. Even when it proves difficult.'

'Probably especially when it proves difficult.' She pursed her lips. 'So, by definition, some of our conversations and discussions are going to be… difficult.'

The colour in his eyes deepened to a green that reminded her of a lagoon in Thailand where they'd spent a lazy afternoon. She swallowed and tried not to linger on what had happened after that swim when Ryan had taken her back to his beach hut.

'You want to hit me with whatever's on your mind?'

She dragged herself back.

The colour in his eyes intensified. 'I swear to you, Marianna, that I mean to do right by our baby. And by you too. I want to make things as easy for you as I can. I don't want you thinking you're in this alone.'

It was a nice sentiment but… She motioned to his plate. 'You can keep eating while I talk.'

The faintest of smiles touched his lips. 'If we're going to have one of those difficult conversations it might be better if I don't. I wouldn't want to choke, now, would I?'

Her lips kicked up into a smile before she managed to pull herself back into line. 'I think there's an enormous difference between being a good father and being a man who holds the title of father.'

'I agree.'

'To be good at anything means working hard at it, don't you think?'

Again, he nodded. 'I'm not afraid of hard work, I promise you.' He met her gaze, his face pale but his eyes steady. 'What I'm afraid of is failure.'

His admission had her breaking out in gooseflesh as her own fears crowded about her. She chafed her arms. 'That's something I can definitely relate to.'

He shook his head. 'You're going to be a brilliant mother. You shouldn't doubt that for a moment. Already you're fighting for your baby's happiness—protecting it.'

But did it need protecting from Ryan?

'You will be a wonderful mother,' he repeated.

Her stomach screwed up tight. She hoped so.

His eyes suddenly narrowed. 'Are you afraid you won't be?'

'No,' she lied. 'Of course not.' She'd be just fine.

She would! Besides, one of them feeling wobbly on the parent front was more than enough, thank you very much.

Ryan folded his arms. 'It hasn't been a terribly difficult discussion so far.'

Ah. Well. She could fix that. She pushed her cake to one side and pressed her hands together. 'Ryan, in Thailand I…' She faltered for a moment before finding her footing again. 'I was coming home to Italy after a year spent travelling and working through Australia. Thailand was my…last hurrah, so to speak. That holiday was about having no responsibilities, being young and free, and living in the moment before settling back into my real life.'

A furrow appeared on his brow. 'I understand that.'

'You are an incredibly attractive man.'

He blinked.

'But what we had in Thailand—all of that glorious sex…' He grinned as if in remembrance and it made her pulse skitter. 'It…it just doesn't belong here in my real world.'

He sobered as he caught her drift.

'If we're to successfully co-parent, then sex has no place in that. Friendship would be great if we can manage it. Sex would wreck that.'

'Too complicated,' he agreed.

She shook her head. 'It's actually incredibly simple. You never want to marry while I'd love to find the man of my dreams and settle down with him. If we make love here—in my real world—I would be in grave danger of falling in love with you.'

He shot back in his seat, his eyes filling with horror. The pulse in his throat pounded. 'I...' He gulped. 'That would be seriously unwise.'

She snorted. 'It'd be a disaster.' And if they were being honest... 'I doubt I'd make a particularly gracious jilted lover.'

He raised both hands. 'Point taken. We keep our hands to ourselves, keep things strictly platonic and...friendship.' He nodded vigorously. 'We focus on friendship.'

Ryan stared at Marianna, his heart doing its best to pound a way out of his chest. There couldn't be any sex between them. *Ever again.* She'd just presented him with his nightmare scenario and... Just, *no*. It would wreck everything.

He swallowed and tried to slow his pulse. If only he could forget the satin slide of her skin or the dancing delight of her fingertips as they travelled across his naked flesh, not to mention the sweet

warm scent of her and the way he'd relished burying his face in her hair and breathing her in.

He stamped a lid on those memories and shoved
them into a vault in his mind marked: *Never to be
opened.*

Marianna lifted another spoonful of cake to her
lips. He glanced at his fettuccine, but pushed the
plate away, his stomach now too acid. Marianna
had told him the food here was superb, world class,
but it could've been sawdust for all he knew.

He glanced across the table and his gaze snagged
hers. 'You really don't mean to make it difficult
for me to see our child?'

Very slowly she shook her head. 'Not if you want
to be involved.'

He wanted to be involved all right. He just didn't
know what *involved* actually entailed. 'So…where
do we go from here?'

She halted with a spoon of cake only centime-
tres from her mouth.

He tried not to focus on her mouth. 'I mean, what
do we do next?'

She lowered her spoon. 'I don't really know. I…'
She frowned and he went on immediate alert. It
had to be better for her health and the baby's if she
smiled rather than frowned.

Also, it had to be seriously bad for her health—her blood pressure—to go about hurling vases at people. He made a mental note to try and defuse all such high emotion in the future.

Her spoon clattered back to her plate and she gestured heavenwards with a dramatic flourish. 'It feels as if there must be a million things to do before the baby arrives!'

Were there? Asking what they were would only reveal the extent of his ignorance. He hadn't been able to shake off her horrified expression when she'd realised he'd never so much as held a baby. So, he didn't ask what needed doing. Instead he asked, 'What can I do?'

She folded her arms and surveyed him. She might only be a petite five feet two inches, but it took all of his strength to not fidget under that gaze.

'You really want to help?'

'Yes.' That was unequivocal. He *needed* to help.

'I plan to move out of the family home and into a cottage on the estate.'

He wondered if her brothers knew about this yet.

'It's solid and hardy, but I'd like to spruce up the inside with a new coat of paint and make everything lovely and fresh for the baby.'

It took a moment before he realised what she was asking of him. His heart started to thud. She'd told him that if he was serious about becoming a good father, his time would no longer be his own. His mouth dried. Could he do this?

He had to do this!

He reviewed his upcoming work schedule. He set his shoulders and rested both arms on the table. 'How would it be if I spent the next month—' *four whole weeks!* '—in Monte Calanetti? I can work remotely with maybe just the odd day trip back to Rome, and in my spare time I can help you get established in your cottage, help you set up a nursery…and in return you can tell me what you see as the duties and responsibilities of a good father?'

Her eyes widened, and he was suddenly fiercely glad he'd made the offer. 'You'd stay for a whole month?'

It wouldn't interfere with the Conti contract, and he didn't kid himself—he'd only have one chance to prove himself to the mother of his yet-to-be-born child, and he wasn't going to waste it. 'Consider it done,' he said.

CHAPTER FOUR

MARIANNA STARED AT him and Ryan found himself holding his breath, waiting for her answer... her verdict.

She folded her arms. 'That would help me out a lot.'

'And me,' he added, wanting her to remember that she'd just promised to tutor him in the arts of fatherhood.

She stared down at her cake and bit her lip. Her hair fell around her shoulders in a riot of dark waves, and it suddenly struck him how young she looked. He pushed his plate further away and glanced at her again. 'How old are you, Marianna?'

'Twenty-four.'

She was so young!

'And you?'

'Twenty-nine.' It was one of the many pieces of information they hadn't exchanged during their week in Thailand.

'If you researched me on the Internet, then you

know what I do for a living.' As a specialist freelance consultant brought in, usually at the last moment, to turn the fortunes of ailing companies around, he enjoyed the adrenaline surge, the high-stakes pressure, and the tight deadlines. He shifted on his seat. 'What about you? What's your role at the vineyard? Are you a winemaker?'

She shook her head and those glorious curls performed a gentle dance around her face and shoulders. 'Nico is the vintner. I'm a viticulturist. I grow the grapes, look after the health of the vines.' She pushed a lock of hair behind her ear. 'The art of grape growing is a science.'

He knew she had a brain. It shouldn't surprise him that she used it. 'Sounds…technical.'

'I grew up on the vineyard. It's in my blood.'

The smile she sent him tightened his skin. He tried to ignore the pulse of sexual awareness coursing through him. That was *not* going to happen. No matter how much he might want her, he wasn't messing with her emotions.

'What?' she said.

He shook himself. 'So your job is stable? Financially you're…secure?'

He could've groaned when her face turned stormy.

He raised both hands. 'No offence meant. Difficult conversations, remember?'

She blew out a breath and slumped back, offered him a tiny smile that speared straight into the centre of him. 'I feel as if you're quizzing me to make sure I'm suitable mother material.'

'*Not* what I'm doing.' He'd be the least qualified person on earth to do that.

She kinked an eyebrow. 'No?'

He shook his head. 'When I said I wanted to make things easier for you, I meant in every way.'

He saw the moment his meaning reached her. The hand she rested on the table—small like the rest of her—clenched. He waited with an internal grimace and a kind of fatalistic inevitability for her to throw something at him.

In amazement he watched as her hand unclenched again. 'I keep forgetting that you don't really know me.'

He knew the shape of her legs, the dip of her waist and the curves of her breasts. He knew the feel of her skin and how she tasted. Hunger rushed through him. He closed his eyes. He had to stop this.

'One thing you ought to know is that I do have my pride.' She pulled in a breath and let it out slowly. 'I have both the means and the wherewithal to take care of myself and—' her hand moved to cover her still-flat stomach '—whoever else comes along. I have a share in Vigneto Calanetti, I'm a qualified viticulturist, I work hard and I draw a good salary. It may not be in the same league as what you earn, Ryan, but it's more than sufficient for both my and the baby's needs. I think you ought to know that if you were to offer me money it would seriously offend me.'

Right. That *was* good to know, but… 'What if I weren't offering it to you, but to the baby?'

She frowned and gestured to his plate. 'Are you finished?' At his nod she glanced across the room and caught the maître d's eye, wordlessly asking for the bill.

He let her distract herself with these things, but this money issue wasn't something he'd let her ignore indefinitely. He had a financial responsibility to this child—a responsibility he was determined to meet. He left a generous tip and followed Marianna to the cobbled street outside. He glanced at her and then glanced around. 'Your village is charming.'

It did what it was supposed to do—it cleared the frown from her face and perked her up. 'This was a stronghold back in medieval times. Many of the stones from the wall have since been used to build the houses that came after, but sections of the wall still stand. Would you like to walk for a bit?'

'I'd like that a lot. If you're not feeling too tired.'

She scoffed at that and set about leading him through cool cobbled streets that wound through the town with a grace that seemed to belong to a bygone age. He found himself entranced with houses made from stone that had mellowed to every shade of rose and gold, with archways leading down quaint alleys that curved intriguingly out of view. There were walled gardens, quirky turrets and fountains in the oddest places. And all the while Marianna pointed out architectural curiosities and regaled him with stories from local folklore. Her skill on the subject surprised him.

It shouldn't. Her quick wit and keen intelligence had been evident from their very first meeting.

Her enthusiasm for her subject made her eyes shine. She gestured with her hands as if they were an extension of her mind. His gut tightened as he watched her. Hunger roared through him…

He wrenched his gaze heavenwards. *For heaven's sake, can't you get your mind off sex for just ten minutes?*

'I'm boring you.'

He swung back to her. 'On the contrary, I'm finding all of this fascinating.' He refused to notice the shape of her lips. 'You obviously love your town.'

'It's my home,' she said simply. 'I love it. I missed it when I was in Australia.' She frowned up at him. 'Don't you love your home?'

Something inside him froze.

Her frown deepened. 'Where *is* your home, Ryan?'

'Have you heard the saying "Wherever I lay my hat, that's my home"? That pretty much sums me up.'

She halted, hands on her hips. 'But you have to live somewhere when you're between assignments. I mean, where do you keep your belongings?'

'I have office facilities in Sydney and London, and staff who work for me in both locations, but...' He shrugged.

Her eyes grew round. 'What? Are you telling me that you just live out of hotel rooms?'

'Suites,' he corrected.

'But—' She frowned. 'What about your car? Where do you keep that?'

'Whenever I need a car, I hire one.'

'Then what about the gifts people give you, your

books and CDs, photographs, art you've gathered and... Oh, I don't know. The myriad things we collect?'

'I travel light. All I need is a suitcase and my laptop.'

She eased away from him, those dark eyes surveying him. 'I wasn't so wrong about you after all,' she finally said. 'You are a kind of gypsy.'

She didn't look too pleased with her discovery. He shrugged. 'While we're on the subject of accommodation, perhaps you could recommend somewhere for me to stay while I'm in Monte Calanetti?'

She folded her arms and frowned at him for a long moment and then tossed her head, eyes flashing. 'Oh, that's easy.' She swung away and led him down an avenue that opened out into a town square. 'If you're going to help me get the cottage shipshape then you can stay there.'

His heart stuttered. 'With you?'

Some of his horror must've seeped into his voice because she swung back with narrowed eyes. 'Do you have a problem with that?'

'Not at all,' he assured her hastily. *Hell, yes!* How on earth was he going to avoid temptation when he was living with her? He rolled his shoulders. Not that he could ask the question out loud. Not when she stood glaring at him like that.

She turned and moved off, sending him a knowing glance over her shoulder. 'Considering the circumstances of our *acquaintance*, local traditions of hospitality demand I offer you a place to stay.'

What on earth was she talking about?

'If you don't stay at the vineyard, Ryan, tongues will wag.'

Ah. He didn't want to make things here in the village uncomfortable for her.

Her lips suddenly twitched. 'Of course, you could always stay in the main house with Angelo and Nico if you prefer.'

'No, no, the cottage will be great.'

She waved to a group of men on the other side of the square before leading Ryan to a bench bathed in warm spring sunshine. The square rose up around them in stone that glowed gold and pink. In the middle of the square stood a stone fountain—a nymph holding aloft a clamshell. It sent a glittering sparkle of water cascading, the fine mist making rainbows in the air. The nearby scent of sautéing onion, garlic and bacon tantalised his nose, reminding him of lunch and the abandoned conversation that he hadn't forgotten.

'In my country, Marianna, it's the law for a man to pay child maintenance to help look after his children. I expect it's the law here too. I *will* be giving you money. It's only right and fair that I contribute financially.'

Her mouth opened but he rushed on before she could speak. 'This is non-negotiable. I insist on contributing to my child's upkeep. I have my pride too.' She tried to butt in but he held up a hand. 'The money is not for you, it's for the baby.'

She folded her arms and slumped back against the bench, dark eyes staring towards the centre of the square. He couldn't help feeling he'd wounded her in some way. It didn't mean he wanted to unsay it. He had every intention of being financially accountable in this situation, but…

'None of that is to say that I believe for a single moment that you're not capable of looking after the baby on your own. Of course you are.'

Those dark eyes met his and he didn't understand the turmoil in their depths. 'Imagine for a moment I was one of your brothers. Wouldn't they want to contribute to the care of their child?'

Very slowly her chin and her shoulders unhitched. 'I suppose you're right.'

He let out a breath he hadn't known he'd been

holding. Being around this woman was like ne-gotiating a minefield. He didn't know from one moment to the next what would set her off. He dragged a hand back through his hair. What on earth had happened to the sweet sunny girl he'd met in Thailand?

She still had the same sweet curves, and when she smiled—

Stop it!

'So…' She pursed those luscious lips of hers and Ryan had to drag his gaze away. 'We've dis-cussed the fact that you want to be involved in the baby's life, that you want to be a good father. We've talked about money, and settled that you're going to stay here in Monte Calanetti for the next month. We've organised where you're going to stay dur-ing that time. Is there anything else we need to tackle today?'

The dark circles beneath her eyes beat at him. He'd put them there. She'd returned here yester-day after their dreadful interview and cried. She'd probably barely slept a wink for worry. *His fault.*

'Maybe we should return to the vineyard. You can put your feet up and relax for a bit and—'

'Oh, for heaven's sake, Ryan, I'm pregnant not an invalid!'

Whoa. Okay. 'I, um…well, maybe I can put my feet up. I'm kind of beat after the drive from Rome.'

She swung to him, her eyes filling with tears. 'Oh, I'm sorry. Of course you're tired. What a dreadful hostess I'm proving to be.'

He prayed her tears wouldn't fall. He didn't want to deal with a sobbing woman. 'You, uh…you don't have to assume any role on my account.' If they were going to make this work then they had to drop pretences.

And he *had* to make it work. He had to learn how to be a good father to this child so that when Marianna found her true love and had more babies, he'd be there when she no longer had time for the cuckoo in the nest.

There was no doubt in his mind that when she did marry and start a new family, this child could be cast aside. She wasn't as young as his mother had been when she'd become pregnant with Ryan, but she was still young. Marianna mightn't see it at the moment, but raising another man's baby would throw a pall over any life she tried to build with a new man. And Ryan vowed to be there for his child when that happened.

* * *

Marianna directed Ryan to park his car beneath the carport standing to one side of the villa—the villa that was her family home. He switched off the ignition and turned to her. 'Have you told your brothers about your plan to move?'

His tone told her he thought she'd have a fight on her hands. She bit back a sigh. Tell her something she didn't know. 'Not yet.'

'Would you like me there when you do?'

'No, thank you.' His earlier non-negotiable 'I'm paying for my child' still stung. Did he think her completely helpless? Did he think her utterly incapable of looking after her baby?

'When are you planning to move in?'

She lifted her chin. 'Tomorrow.' And nobody was going to stop her. But…

Pushing out of the car, she bit back a curse. What on earth had possessed her to offer him a room at the cottage? How relaxing was that going to be? *Not.*

She passed a hand across her forehead. It was just… She'd been utterly horrified when she'd learned how he lived his life. How could someone have no home? What kind of upbringing had this man had to have him still shunning the idea of a home?

If he wanted to co-parent he would need to create a home for their child, and she wanted him to experience at least a little of the welcoming atmosphere of a real home. If he helped her to create that warm environment perhaps he could emulate it.

Unless he had his heart set on sticking to hotel rooms. *Suites.* Would a baby mind…or even notice? Heavens, a toddler would have a field day!

When she turned back to face him, however, it wasn't their child's welfare that occupied her thoughts. It was his. Her heart burned for him and she couldn't explain why, but for as long as he stayed here in Monte Calanetti she wanted to wipe away the memories of all of those impersonal anonymous hotel rooms and replace them with warmth and belonging.

Which, of course, made no sense at all.

Think with your head, not your heart.

You're too impulsive.

Those were the voices of her brothers.

She reached up to scratch between her shoulder blades. Maybe it was simply pregnancy hormones making her feel maternal early or something.

Speaking of hormones… She thought back to

some of her reactions during lunch and grimaced. She wasn't exactly doing a great job at holding her emotions in check at the moment, was she?

Do you really think you can blame that on pregnancy hormones?

She flinched. Maybe she was as immature and irresponsible as her brothers seemed to think. Maybe she had no right becoming a mother. Maybe she'd be a terrible mother—

'What's wrong?'

She blinked to find Ryan right beside her. How had he known anything was wrong? She hadn't even been facing him. How could he be so attuned to her when he didn't really know her?

But he does know you. He knows every inch of your body intimately.

She gulped. *Don't think about that now.*

'Marianna.' He smoothed her hair back from her face before clasping her shoulders. 'If you're afraid of your brothers, then let me inform them of your intentions. I'll do anything you need me to.'

Except marry me.

That had her jerking out of his grip. She *didn't* want to marry him. 'I'm not afraid of Angelo and Nico, Ryan. It's just…I…' She spun away, swore and spun back. 'I feel as if I have constant PMS—

as if some alien has taken over my mind and is making me behave irrationally. And it's taken over my body too. My breasts hurt. If I cross my arms, it hurts. If I reach up to get something from a shelf, it hurts. Putting a seat belt on is an exercise in agony, and I'm not even going to talk about the torture of putting on a bra. I…it's making me tetchy. And then I feel like I'm some kind of immature loser who can't deal with a bit of breast tenderness and some whacky hormones, and who's creating a whole lot of trouble for everyone else.'

She paused, running out of breath and Ryan's jaw dropped. 'Why didn't you say something earlier?'

'Because—' she ground her teeth together '—I should be bigger than it.'

'Garbage!' He reached out and cupped her face. 'I would hug you only I don't want to hurt you.' The sweet sincerity in his eyes melted something inside her. 'But let me tell you now that you're not a loser. You're warm and beautiful and brave.'

He thought her beautiful?

So that's the bit—out of all that he just said— that you latch onto, is it? Very mature.

She tried to ignore that critical inner voice.

'I don't feel brave,' she murmured. She didn't feel beautiful either, but she left that unsaid.

'I think you're wonderfully brave. I also think it understandable for you to be worried about the future. You shouldn't beat yourself up about that.'

'Okay,' she whispered.

With that, he drew away. She missed his touch, the brief connection they'd seemed to share. She shook it off and made herself smile. 'C'mon, I'll show you the cottage.'

'You want to do what?' Angelo shouted from where he set the table.

She bit back a sigh. The moment she'd informed her brothers that Ryan was coming to dinner, Angelo had cancelled his date with Kayla, and Nico had returned earlier than normal from the vineyard with a martial light in his eye. She'd figured, *In for a penny...*

'That's ridiculous!' Angelo slammed down the last knife and fork. 'Nico, talk sense into the girl.'

Marianna doggedly tossed the salad from her post at the kitchen bench.

'Mari—' Nico swung from where he turned steaks on the grill. '*This* is your home. *This* is where you belong.'

She turned at that. 'No, Nico, this is *your* home.' One day he'd fill it with a wife and children of his own, but his head rocked back at her words and he turned white. Her head bled a little for him. 'Turn the steaks,' she ordered and he did as she bid. 'I don't mean that as some kind of denial or as an indication that I don't feel welcome here. This is my childhood home. It will always be a haven for me. If I need it. Currently, though, I don't need a haven.'

'But—'

'No!' She spun back to Angelo. 'Do *you* feel as if this is your home? When you marry your beautiful Kayla, do *you* mean to settle in this house?'

He rolled his shoulders. 'That's different.'

'Why?' she fired back at him. 'Because you're a man?'

'Because I haven't lived here in years! I've built a different life for myself.'

'And what's wrong with me building a different life for myself?'

'Marianna,' Nico spluttered. 'You *do* belong here! You play a key role at Vigneto Calanetti—'

'But it doesn't mean I have to live under this roof. I'll still be living on the estate.'

Both brothers started remonstrating again. Marianna tossed the salad for all she was worth while she waited for them to wear themselves out. It had always been this way. She'd make a bid for independence, they'd rail at her, telling her why it was a bad idea and forbidding her to do it—whatever *it* might be—they'd eventually calm down, and then she'd go ahead and do it anyway.

Their overprotectiveness was a sign of their love for her. She knew that. They'd had more of a hand in raising her than their parents. But there was no denying that they could get suffocating at times.

'Enough!'

The voice came from the French doors. *Ryan.* She glanced around to find him framed in the doorway—all broad and bristling and commanding. Her blood did a cha-cha-cha. She swallowed and waved him inside, hoping no one noticed how her hand shook. 'You're right on time.'

He strode up to her side. 'Leave Marianna be. The one thing she doesn't need is to be bullied by the pair of you.'

'Bullied?' Nico spluttered.

'Who are you to tell us what to do?' Angelo said in a deceptively soft voice.

Ryan turned his gaze on her eldest brother—a determined intense glare that made her heart beat harder. 'I'm the father of her unborn child, that's who. And I'm telling you now that she doesn't need all of this…high drama.'

Her brothers blinked and she had to bite back a laugh. Normally it was she who was accused of the high drama.

It was her turn to blink when he took her shoulders in his hands and propelled her around the kitchen bench into the nearest chair at the dining table. 'Oh, but I was tossing the salad!'

He glanced at the bowl and his lips twitched. 'Believe me, that salad is well and truly tossed.' But he brought the bowl over and set it on the table in front of her.

Angelo glanced into the bowl and grimaced. 'You trying to mangle it?'

She bit her lip. Perhaps she had been a little enthusiastic on the tossing front.

'It looks great,' Ryan assured her.

The fibber! But it made her feel better all the same.

Angelo shook himself up into 'protective big brother' mode. 'Are you supporting my sister in this crazy scheme of hers to move out of the family home?'

'I'm supporting Marianna's right to assert her

independence, to live wherever she chooses and to build the home she wants to for her child.'

'And *your* child,' Nico said, bringing the steaks across to the table.

'And my child,' Ryan agreed, not waiting to be told where to sit, but planting himself firmly in the seat beside Marianna.

'Are you planning to marry?'

Ryan glared at both of her brothers. 'You want Marianna to marry a man she doesn't love?'

Both Angelo and Nico glanced away.

Her shoulders started to slump. Why wouldn't they believe she could take care of herself? Maybe if she didn't have such a dreadful dating track record...?

She shook herself upright again, took the platter of steaks and placed a portion on each of their plates. She then handed the bowl of salad to Ryan, as their guest, to serve himself first. He didn't, though. He served out the salad to her plate first, and then his own before passing the bowl across the table to Nico. He seized the basket of bread and held it out for her to select one of the warmed rolls.

Her brothers noted all of this through narrowed eyes. Marianna lifted her chin. 'Ryan is going to stay here for a bit while we sort out how we mean to arrange things.'

Nico's eyes narrowed even further. He glared at Ryan. 'Where precisely will you be staying?'

Marianna rounded on him. 'Don't speak to him like that! Ryan is my guest. For as long as he's in Monte Calanetti he'll be staying at the cottage with me.'

Her brothers' eyes flashed.

Ryan drew himself up to his full seated height. 'Marianna and I might have decided against marriage, but I have an enormous amount of respect for your sister. I...' He shrugged. 'I like her.'

She blinked. Really? But... He barely knew her.

Still, if he could claim to like her after she'd thrown a vase of flowers at his head, and sound as if he meant it, then...who knew? Maybe he did like her.

'We're friends.'

'Pshaw!' Angelo slashed a disgusted hand through the air. 'If Mari hadn't become pregnant you'd have never clapped eyes on her again. That's not my idea of friendship.'

'But she is pregnant. I *am* the father of her child. We're now a team.'

Marianna speared a piece of cucumber and

brought it to her mouth. A team? That sounded nice. 'Please, guys, will you eat before your steaks get cold?'

The three men picked up their cutlery.

'Still,' Nico grumbled. 'This is a fine pickle the two of you have landed in.'

Ryan halted from slicing into his steak. 'This is not a pickle. Granted, Marianna's pregnancy wasn't planned, but she's having a baby. She's bringing a new life into the world. That is a cause for celebration and joy, *not* recriminations.'

Her eyes filled as he repeated her sentiment from earlier in the day.

Ryan took her hand. 'Do you think your sister won't be a wonderful mother?'

'She'll be a fabulous mother, of course,' Nico said.

'Do you not think it'll be a joyous thing to have a nephew or niece?'

'Naturally, when Marianna's *bambino* arrives, it will be cause for great celebration.' Angelo rolled his shoulders and then a smile touched his lips. 'I am looking forward to teaching my nephew how to play catch.'

'No, no, Angelo, we will have to teach him how to kick a ball so he can go on to play for Fiorentina.'

She rolled her eyes at Nico's mention of his and Angelo's favourite football team.

'What will you teach him?' Angelo challenged.

'Cricket.' Ryan thrust out his jaw. 'I'm going to teach him how to play cricket like a champion.'

'Cricket! That's a stupid sport. I—'

'And what if my *bambino* is a girl?' Marianna said, breaking into the male posturing, but she too found herself gripped with the sudden excitement of having a child. Her brothers would make wonderful uncles. They'd dote on her child and if she weren't careful they'd spoil it rotten.

'A girl can play soccer,' Nico said.

'And cricket,' Ryan added.

'She might like a pony,' Angelo piped in.

Her jaw dropped. 'You wouldn't let *me* get a pony when I wanted one.'

'I was afraid you'd try and jump the first fence you came across and break your neck.' Angelo shook his head. 'Mari, it was hard enough keeping up with you when you were powered by your own steam. It would've been explosive to add anything additional to the mix.' His eyes danced for a moment. 'Besides, if you do have a daughter and if she does get a pony, it'll be your responsibility to keep up with her. Something you'll manage on your ear, no doubt.'

She found herself suddenly beaming. Nico laughed and it hit her then that Ryan had accomplished this. He'd made her brothers—and her—excited at the prospect of their new arrival. He'd channelled their fear and worry into this—a new focus on the positive.

Reaching beneath the table, she squeezed his hand in thanks. He gazed at her blankly and she realised that he hadn't a clue what he'd done. She released him again with a sigh.

'Okay, Paulo,' Angelo said grudgingly. 'You're at least saying the right things. Still, in my book actions speak louder than words. I'll be watching you.'

Marianna rolled her eyes. Ryan shrugged as if completely unaffected by the latent threat lacing her brother's words. He glanced across at Nico. 'Anything you'd like to add?'

Nico stared at him with his dark steady eyes. 'I will abide by Marianna's wishes. You can stay. But I don't trust you.'

Marianna's stomach screwed up tight then and started to churn. She didn't know if she could trust him or not either.

Ryan's mobile phone chose that moment to ring. He pulled it from his pocket and glanced at the display. 'I'm sorry, but I have to take this.'

But...but...he was supposed to be making a good impression on her brothers!

With barely a glance of apology, he rose and strode out to the terrace, phone pressed to his ear.

He was supposed to be learning how to be a good father!

Lone wolf. The words went round and round in her mind. Was this how the next month would go? Ryan claiming he was invested and committed to their child, but leaping into work mode every time his phone rang? Her brothers stared at her with hard eyes. 'Excuse me.' Pressing a hand to her mouth, she fled for the bathroom.

CHAPTER FIVE

FOR THE NEXT three days, Ryan kept himself busy alternating between conference calls and prepping the inside walls of the three-bedroom stone cottage that Marianna had her heart set on calling home. In her parents' time, apparently, it had been used as a guesthouse and before that it had been the head vintner's cottage. For the last few years, however, the cottage had stood empty.

Ryan had insisted on cleaning everything first— mopping and vacuuming—before Marianna moved in. She'd grumbled something about being more than capable of wielding a mop, but he'd ordered her off the premises. Cleaning seemed the least he could do, even if it had delayed her move for an additional day. He'd claimed the smallest of the three bedrooms as his for the next month.

As Marianna had spent what he assumed was a long day tending grapevines and whatever else it was that she did, Ryan cooked dinner.

She walked in, found him stir-frying vegetables,

and folded her arms. 'Do you also think me incapable of cooking dinner?'

He thought women were supposed to like men who cooked and cleaned. Not that he wanted her to like him. At least, not like *that*. 'Of course not, but I don't expect you to do all the cooking while I'm here. I thought we could take it turn about. You can cook tomorrow night.'

She grumbled something in Italian that he was glad he didn't understand. Throwing herself down on the sofa, she rifled through the stack of magazines on the coffee table and settled back with one without another word.

He stared at the previously *neat* stack. He itched to march over there to tidy them back up, but a glance at Marianna warned him to stay right where he was.

Dinner was a strained affair. 'Bad day at work?' he asked.

'I've had better.'

Something inside him tightened. Had her brothers been hassling her again? He opened his mouth, but the tired lines around her eyes had him closing it again. His hands clenched and unclenched in his lap. What he should do was wash the dishes and then retreat to his room to do some work. Work was something he could do—something he had a handle on and was good at. He glanced at Marianna, grimaced at the way her mouth drooped, and with a silent curse pulled his laptop towards him. 'I thought maybe you could choose the colours for the walls.' He clicked on the screen, bringing up a colour chart.

The entire cottage oozed quaint cosy charm. The main living-dining area was a single room—long and low—with the kitchen tucked in one corner, sectioned off from the rest of the room by a breakfast nook. The ceiling was low-beamed, which should've made the room dark, but a set of French doors off the dining area, opening to a small walled garden, flooded the room with light. The garden was completely overgrown, of course, but if a body had a mind to they could create a great herb garden out there.

'Colour charts?' Marianna perked up, pushing her plate aside. 'That sounds like fun.'

Colour charts fun? That was a new one, but he'd go with it if it put a bit of colour back into her cheeks. He removed their plates as unobtrusively as he could. Hesitating on his way back from the kitchen, he detoured past the coffee table and swooped down to straighten the stack of magazines before easing into the seat beside Marianna at the dining table again.

She moved the laptop so he could see it too. 'That one.' She pointed to a particularly vivid yellow. 'I've always wanted a yellow kitchen.'

He glanced at the screen and then at her. Did she really want a yellow so intense it glowed neon? 'That one's really bright.'

'I know. Gorgeous, isn't it?'

'Um… I'm thinking it might be a tad brighter on your walls than you realise.'

'Or it could be perfect.'

He didn't doubt for a moment she'd hate the colour once it was on her walls, but a colour scheme wasn't worth arguing about—especially if she was feeling a bit testy and—his gaze dropped momentarily to her breasts—sore. He reefed his gaze back to the computer screen. He'd paint her walls pink and purple stripes if she wanted. Pulling in a breath, he reconciled himself to the fact he'd be repainting said wall at some stage in the future. 'Butter Ball, right.' He made a note.

He'd started to twig to the fact that there were two Mariannas. There was the sunny, sassy Marianna he partially recognised from his holiday in Thailand. And then there was 'crazy pregnant lady' Marianna. She swung between these extremes with no rhyme or reason—sunny one moment and all snark and growl the next.

It kept a man on his toes.

'You mentioned you wanted some sort of green in the living and dining areas.' He glanced around. At the moment they were a nice inoffensive cream. With a shake of his head, he clicked to bring up a green palette. Heaven only knew what hideous colour she'd sentence him to using next.

She leaned in closer to peer at the screen, drenching him in the scent of…frangipani? Whatever it was, it was sweet and flowery and so fresh it took all his strength not to lean over and breathe her in all the more deeply.

'It'll have a name like olive or sage or something,' she said. 'Hmm…that one.'

He forced his attention back to the screen. 'Sea foam,' he read. It was a lot better than he'd been expecting.

'Does *it* pass muster?'

He didn't like the martial light in her eye. *Deflect the snark.* 'It's perfect.'

She blinked. Her shoulders slumped and he had to fight the urge to give her a hug. 'How are your breasts?'

She stiffened and then shot away from him with a glare. '*I beg your pardon?* What have my breasts to do with *you*?'

Heat crept up his neck. 'I didn't mean it in a salacious, pervy kind of way. It's just…the other day you said they were sore and…and I was just hoping that…that it had settled down.'

'Why should you care?' she all but yelled at him, leaping up to pace around the table and then the length of the room. She flung out an arm. 'You're probably happy! I've inconvenienced you so I expect you're secretly pleased to see me suffer.'

He stood too. 'Then you'd be spectacularly wrong! I have absolutely no desire to see you suffer. Ideally, what I want is you happy and healthy.'

She stopped dead in the middle of the room and stared at him, her hands pressed together at her waist. Ryan pulled in a breath. 'It's obvious, though, that at the moment you're not happy.'

Where did that leave him and her?

Where did it leave the baby? If she were having second thoughts about keeping the child…

She swallowed. Her bottom lip wobbled for a fraction of a sentence. Her vulnerability tugged at him. 'If I'm the cause of that, if my living here in your cottage, and invading your space, is adding to your stress, then I can easily move into the village. It wouldn't be a big deal and—'

He broke off when she backed up to drop down onto the sofa, covered her face with her hands and burst into tears.

He brought his fist to his mouth. Hell! He hadn't meant to make her cry. He shifted his weight from one foot to the other before kicking himself into action and lurching over to the sofa to put an arm around her. 'I'm sorry, Mari. I didn't mean to upset you. I'm a clumsy oaf—no finesse.'

At his words she turned her face into his chest and sobbed harder. He wrapped both arms around her, smoothed a hand up and down her back in an attempt to soothe her. Protectiveness rose up through him and all but tried to crush him. He fought back an overwhelming sense of suffocation. At the moment he had to focus on making Marianna feel better. His discomfiture had no bearing on anything. Her health and the baby's health, they were what mattered.

Eventually her sobs eased. She rested against him and he could feel the exhaustion pounding through her. So far this week all his suggestions that she rest had been met with scorn, sarcasm and a flood of vindictive Italian. Now he kept his mouth firmly closed on the subject.

'I'm sorry,' she whispered.

She eased away from him and her pallor made him wince.

'I can't believe I said something so mean to you, Ryan. I didn't mean it. It was dreadfully unfair. I know you don't want to see me suffer.'

'It's okay. It doesn't matter.'

'It's *not* okay. And it *does* matter.' Her voice, though vehement, was pitched low. 'I don't know what's happening to me. I'm being so awful to everyone. Today at work when I was lifting a bag of supplies, Tobias came rushing over to take it from me.'

She was heavy lifting at work!

'I mean, I know he meant well, but I just let fly at him in the most awful way. I apologised later, of course, but Tobias has worked for my family for twenty years. He deserves nothing from me except respect and courtesy. And now I'm going out of my way to be extra nice to him to try and make amends and…this is terrible to admit, but it's exhausting.'

He could imagine, but… *She was heavy lifting at work?*

'And then I come home here and you've been working on my lovely cottage and am I grateful? No, not a bit of it!' She stiffened and then swung to him. 'I mean, I *am* grateful. Truly I am. But how on earth are you to know that when I keep acting like a shrew?'

Her earnestness made him smile. 'I know you are.'

She shook her head, her wild curls fizzing up all around her. 'How can you possibly know that when all I do is yell and say cruel things? I'm so sorry, Ryan. Even as I'm saying them a part of me is utterly appalled, but I can't seem to make myself stop. I just...' She swallowed. 'I don't know what's wrong with me.'

'I do.'

She stared at him. She folded her arms. 'You do?'

He tried not to let her incredulity sting. 'It's not that there's anything wrong with you. It's just your body is being flooded with pregnancy hormones. What you're feeling is natural. I read about it on the Net.'

She straightened. 'I should be able to deal with hormones. I should be able to get the better of them and not let them rule me.'

'Why? When your breasts are feeling sore, can

you magically wish that soreness away just by con-
centrating hard?'

'Well, of course not, but that's different.'

'It's exactly the same,' he countered. 'It's a physical symptom, just like morning sickness.' From
what he could tell, pregnancy put a woman's body
completely through the wringer. He wished he
could share some of the load with her, or carry it
completely, to spare her the upheaval it was caus-
ing.

'So...' She moistened her lips. 'It'll pass?'

'Yep.'

'When?'

Ah, that was a little more difficult to nail down.
She groaned as if reading that answer in his face.
'What am I going to do? If I keep going on like
this I'm not going to have any friends left.'

It was an exaggeration, but it probably felt like
gospel truth to her. He aimed for light. 'I could lock
you up here in the cottage until it passes.'

Her lips twitched. 'It's one solution,' she agreed.
'My brothers, though, might take issue with that
approach.' A moment later she bit back a sigh that
speared straight into his gut. 'I guess I'm just going
to have to ride it out.'

He stood, lifted her feet so that she lay lengthwise on the sofa, and moved across to grab his laptop. 'There're a couple of things we can try.' He came back and crouched down next to the coffee table. 'Meditation is supposed to help.'

She rose up on her elbows. 'Meditation?'

He gestured for her to lie back down. 'I downloaded a couple of guided meditations in case you wanted to try one to see if you thought it might help.'

'Oh.' She lay back down. 'Okay.'

He clicked play and trickling water and birdcalls started to sound. He moved back towards the dining table.

'Ryan?'

He swung back.

'Thank you.'

'You're welcome.'

She shook her head. 'I mean for everything. For understanding and not holding my horridness against me. You're really lovely, you know that?'

His throat thickened.

'I don't want you to move into the village, okay? It's nice to have…a friend here.'

A low melodic voice from his computer instructed her to close her eyes and she did, not waiting for his reply. Which was just as well because he wasn't sure he could utter a single word if his life depended on it.

He moved to sit at the dining table and suddenly realised that with his laptop already in use, he had nothing to do—couldn't lose himself in work as he'd meant to do. Pursing his lips, he glanced around. He'd start the dishes except he didn't want the clattering to disturb her.

Biting back a sigh, he pulled a magazine towards him—some kind of interior decorating magazine that Marianna must've picked up at some point… and left lying around the place. Instead of focusing on the magazine, though, he found his attention returning again and again to the woman on the sofa. He clocked the exact moment she fell asleep. He tiptoed across to cover her with a throw blanket, before moving straight back to his seat at the table where he wouldn't be in danger of reaching out to trace a finger down the softness of her cheek.

No touching. She'd said it was nice having a friend. He had to work on being that friend. Just a friend.

She slept for an hour. He registered the exact moment she woke too. 'How are you feeling?' he asked when she turned her head in his direction.

She stretched her arms back behind her head. 'Good. Really good.'

She sat up and smiled and he knew he had sunny Marianna back for the moment. He gestured. 'I've been looking through your magazines at the pictures you have marked.'

She leapt up, grabbed a jug of water from the fridge and poured them both a glass before moving across to where he sat. She left the jug on the bench top. He forced himself to stay in his seat and to not go and put it back in the fridge.

'Do you like any of them?'

He dragged his gaze from the offending jug and nodded. She had great taste. If one discounted that awful yellow she'd chosen for the kitchen walls.

She moistened her lips, not meeting his eye. 'Did you look at the pictures of the nurseries?'

Those were the ones he was looking at now. He angled the magazine so she could see. Her eyes went soft. 'They're lovely, aren't they?'

His heart started to hammer in his chest. Never in a million years had he thought he'd be looking at pictures of nurseries. He ran a finger around the collar of his T-shirt. 'Have you decided what kind of style and colour scheme you want in there yet?'

'I can't make up my mind between a nice calm

colour that'll aid sleep or something vibrant that'll stimulate the imagination. I've been researching articles on the topic.'

Her enthusiasm made him smile. 'You're putting a lot of thought into this.'

She pushed her hair behind her ears. 'It's important and…'

'And?'

'I want my—our—baby to be happy. I want to give it every possible advantage I can.'

He stared at her. How long would their baby's welfare be important to her, though?

'Do you have any thoughts?'

Her question pulled him back. 'Personally I'd go for a calm colour because that's what I'd like best. I don't know what a baby would prefer.' He frowned. 'You could go with a calm colour on the walls and brighten the room up with a striking decal and a colourful mobile and…and accessories, couldn't you?'

'Hmm…' she mused. 'The best of both worlds perhaps?'

It warmed something inside him that she took his suggestion seriously. Still… What did he know? He knew nothing about this parenthood caper. 'It seems to me one needs a lot of equipment for a baby.'

'Ooh, yes, I know.' She rubbed her hands together, her eyes dancing. 'Shopping for the baby is going to be so much fun.'

Shopping in his experience was a necessary evil, not fun. Speaking of which... 'Marianna, where will I find the closest hardware store?'

'Ah.' She nodded.

He didn't point out that *Ah* wasn't an answer. He wanted Sunny Marianna hanging around for as long as possible.

'What do you have planned for Saturday?' she asked.

That was the day after tomorrow. He considered his work schedule. He had two video-conferencing calls tomorrow plus a detailed report to write by the end of next week. Saturday he'd planned... He glanced back at Marianna and gestured to the cottage. 'I was hoping to be painting by then.'

'Have you ever been to Siena?'

He shook his head. If that was where the nearest hardware store was, then he hoped it wasn't too far away.

'It's only an hour away. Write up a list of things that we need and we'll make a day of it.'

'Right.' Shopping. Yay.

Her smile slowly dissolved. She stared at him, twisting her hands together for a bit and he hoped he hadn't let his lack of enthusiasm show. He found a smile. 'Sounds good.'

Her fingers moved to worry at the collar of her shirt. She half grimaced, half squinted at him. 'Ryan, do you want to be present at the birth?'

He froze. Um…

'There's an information evening about…stuff coming up soon.'

How on earth had they gone from shopping to the birth? 'What stuff?'

'Like birthing classes.'

He didn't know what to say.

'I'm going to need a birthing partner.'

It became suddenly hard to breathe. 'Are you asking me to be your birthing partner?' What kind of time commitment would that demand?

Her eyes narrowed. 'No. I'm asking you to attend an information evening so we'll have all the available facts and can then make an informed decision about birthing classes and who I might want present at the labour.'

He thought about it. It didn't seem like much to ask. 'Right.' He nodded.

Her hands went to her hips. 'Is that a yes or a no?'

'It's a—yes I'll attend the information evening. When is it?'

'This Monday. Six-thirty.'

He pulled out his phone and put it in his electronic diary. He slotted the phone back into his pocket. 'Got it.'

'The town centre is heritage-listed,' Marianna said, gesturing around the Piazza del Campo. This was the real reason she'd brought Ryan to Siena—to have him experience something spectacular in an effort to make up for all he'd had to put up with from her for the last few days. So much for her resolve to give him a homey, welcoming environment. She'd been acting like a temperamental diva. He'd been incredibly patient and *adult* in the face of it.

Not to mention controlled. She bit back a sigh. If only she could channel some of that control.

Now, though, she had the satisfaction of seeing his eyes widen as he completed a slow circle on the spot to take in the full beauty and splendour of the town square. 'It's amazing.'

'Would you like to see the *duomo*?' Siena Cathedral. 'It's a three-minute walk away.'

At his nod, she led him across the Piazza del Campo and down one of the shady avenues on the other side, detailing a little of the history of the city for him, before eventually leading him to the cathedral.

They gazed at the medieval façade for a long moment, neither saying a word. Eventually Marianna led him through one of the smaller side doors and had the satisfaction of hearing his swift intake of breath. White and greenish-black marble stripes alternated on the walls and columns, creating a magnificent backdrop for the cool and hushed interior. She watched him as he studied everything with a concentrated interest that reminded her of the way he'd explored the underwater wonders of Thailand on their scuba-diving expeditions. It reminded her of the way he'd explored her body during those warm fragrant evenings afterwards.

Something inside her shifted.

Catching her breath, she tried to hitch it back into place. Over and over in her mind she silently recited: *Do not fall for him. Do not fall for him.*

She couldn't fall for Ryan. It had the potential to ruin everything. It had the potential to ruin her child's relationship with him and she couldn't risk that.

She lifted her chin. She *wouldn't* risk that. It'd be selfish, wilful and wrong. What she could do, though, was give Ryan a taste of home and hearth, a sense of how family worked. That was what would be best for their baby.

She turned to look at him and snorted. Fall for him? Not likely. She could never fall for someone so controlled, someone so cold.

He wasn't like that in Thailand.

Maybe not, but that was an aberration, remember?

'What's wrong?'

She snapped to, to find him staring at her. She dredged up a smile, reminding herself she wanted today to be a treat for him. 'Nothing, it's just...' She glanced around the medieval church. 'I've been here many times, but it amazes me all over again each time I come back.'

The smile he sent her warmed her to her very toes. 'I can see why.'

They spent two and a half hours wandering around the city and exploring its sights, and Marianna did her best to be cordial and friendly... and nothing more. After a leisurely lunch, though, Ryan reverted to the colder, more distant version of himself. 'We do need to get supplies at some stage today.'

She bit back a sigh. 'There's a hardware store not too far from where we parked the car.'

'Have you chosen what colour you want for the nursery yet?' he asked when they walked into the store a little while later.

She shook her head. She hadn't settled on anything to do with the nursery. In fact, she found herself strangely reluctant to decorate said nursery with Ryan.

'What?' he said.

She realised she was staring at him. 'I…I'm wondering if I shouldn't leave it and wait until I've had my scan.' She glanced around and then headed down an aisle.

He followed hot on her heels. 'Scan?'

'Hmm… If I find out whether I'm having a boy or a girl maybe that will make it easier to personalise the room.'

He didn't say anything and when she turned to gaze up at him she couldn't read a single emotion in his face. It worried her, though she couldn't have said why.

'You mean to find out the gender of the baby?'

She couldn't work out if that was censure or curiosity in his voice. 'I…I, uh, hadn't made a decision about that yet. There's no denying it'd make things like decorating and buying clothes easier.'

'You don't want it to be a surprise?'

She peered down her nose at him. 'Ryan, don't you think there's been enough of a surprise factor surrounding this pregnancy already?'

He laughed and it eased something inside her. 'Perhaps you're right.'

'If you don't want to know the sex of the baby, then I can keep it a secret.'

He cocked an eyebrow. 'You think that's going to work?'

A chill hand wrapped around her heart. Did he think he could read her so easily?

Her heart started to thump. Maybe he could. She had a tendency to wear her heart on her sleeve while he—he could be utterly inscrutable.

'If I'm doing the majority of the decorating, don't you think your choice of colour schemes is going to give the game away?'

The hand clutching her heart relaxed. 'I could decorate the nursery on my own.'

'You're pregnant. You should be taking it easy.'

She loved that excuse when it came to ducking

out of the dishes, but… 'Slapping on a coat of paint can't be that hard.'

One broad shoulder lifted and a little thrill shot through her at its breadth, its latent strength…its utter maleness. Her mouth started to water. *No thrills!*

'But you may as well make use of me while you have me.'

With an abrupt movement, she turned and marched across to an aisle full of decorative decals. It would be unwise to forget that he was only here for a month. And that he hadn't promised her anything more than help decorating her house. She ground her teeth together. If she could just get her darn hormones under control…

She pulled in a breath and willed the tightness from her body. 'If you wish to remain in suspense as to our baby's sex we best go with something neutral.'

'I didn't say that I didn't want to know.'

She left off staring at teddy bear decals to swing around to him, planting her hands on her hips. 'Well, do you or don't you?'

'I, um…I don't know.'

Helpful. *Not.* She didn't say that out loud, though.

She'd been doing her best to aim for pleasant and rational and she had no intention of failing now.

'I…I kind of feel you've sprung this on me. Not your fault,' he added hastily, as if he thought his admission would have her losing her temper and hurling something at him. 'Can I think about it?'

She shrugged. 'Sure.' She could hardly blame him for feeling all at sea. This was uncharted territory and she felt exactly the same way. She pulled out one of the rolls. 'This is nice, isn't it?'

He took it from her and frowned. 'You can't use this in a boy's room.'

'Why on earth not? It has teddy bears. Teddy bears aren't gender specific. And it's not pink.' It gleamed in the most beautiful shades of ochre and gold.

'It has unicorns.'

'And…?'

He put the roll back on the shelf. 'Believe me, unicorns are a girl thing.' He picked up a different decal displaying jungle animals. 'What about this?'

She pointed. 'The tiger looks a bit fierce. I don't want to give the baby nightmares.'

He put it back and she found she didn't want to talk about nurseries any more, though if pressed she couldn't have said why. She'd been so excited at the prospect yesterday, but...

Before he could reach for another roll she said, 'Can I spring something else on you?'

He halted and then very slowly turned to face her. 'What?'

'I'm having that scan next week. Would you like to come along?'

'I've a few meetings next week.' His face closed up. 'I may even need to spend a day back in Rome, but if I'm free I'll be more than happy to drive you anywhere you need to go.'

'That's not what I meant, Ryan. I have a car. I can drive myself. What I'm asking is if you'd like to be present during the scan.'

He took a step back. 'I don't think...' He looked as if he wanted to turn and flee, but he set himself as if readying for a blow. 'What do you need me to do? What would you like me to do?'

She had to swallow back the ache that rose in her throat. 'It doesn't matter.' But it did. It mattered a lot.

'Then I'll just hang out in the waiting room until you're done.'

He didn't want to see the first pictures of his child, didn't want to hear its heartbeat? She turned from him to run her fingers along the decals, but she didn't see them. 'Ryan, do you love this baby yet?'

She glanced around at his quick intake of breath. He regarded her as if trying to work out what she wanted to hear and she shook her head. 'Honesty, remember? We promised to be honest with each other.'

His shoulders slumped a fraction. A passer-by wouldn't have noticed, but Marianna did. 'It still doesn't feel real to me,' he finally admitted.

She already loved this baby with a fierce protectiveness that took her completely off guard.

'You do.'

His words weren't a question, but a statement. She nodded. 'I expect it's different for a woman. The baby is growing inside of me—it's affecting me physically. That makes it feel very real.' Her stomach constricted at his stricken expression. 'I've also had more time to get used to the idea than you have, Ryan. There was no right or wrong answer to my question.' Just as long as he loved their baby once it arrived. That was all she asked.

He would, wouldn't he? It wouldn't just be a duty?

She reached up to scratch between her shoulder

blades. 'How about we shelve the nursery for another day and focus on the things we need for the rest of the cottage?'

'Right.' He nodded. But he was quiet the entire time they bought paint, brushes, drop sheets and all the other associated paraphernalia one needed for painting. Marianna kept glancing at him, but she couldn't read his mood. While his expression remained neutral, she sensed turmoil churning beneath the surface.

'What next?' he asked when they'd stowed their purchases in the car.

'Soft furnishings.'

She waited for him to make an excuse to go and do something else and arrange to meet up again in an hour. He didn't. He said, 'Lead the way.'

Wow. Okay.

He didn't huff out so much as a single exaggerated sigh while endlessly shifting and fidgeting either. He didn't overtly quell yawns meant to inform her of his boredom, as her brothers would've done. He simply stacked the items she chose into the trolley he pushed, giving his opinion when she asked for it.

He had good taste too.

They moved from bedding to cushions and

tablecloths and finally to curtains. 'They're just not right!' she finally said, tossing a set of curtains back to the shelf.

'What are you looking for?'

'Kitchen curtains. You know, the ones with the bit at the top and then…' She made vague hand gestures.

'Café curtains?'

She stared at him. 'Um…'

He rifled through the selections. 'Like these?'

'That style yes, but the print is hideous.'

'What kind of material are you after?'

She marched over to the store's fabric section and pulled out a roll with a print of orange and lime daisies. 'This is perfect.' A sudden thought struck her. 'Ooh, I wonder if I could find somebody to make them for me? I—'

'I can.'

'And then I—' She stopped dead. She moistened her lips and glanced around at him. 'Did you just say…' no, she couldn't have heard him right '…that you could make me a pair of curtains?'

'That's right.'

'You can sew?'

He nodded.

'How? Why?'

'I had a grandmother who loved to sew.'

He shuffled his feet and glanced away. She did her best to remake her expression into one of friendly interest rather than outright shock. 'She taught you to sew?'

He rolled his shoulders, glancing back at her with hooded eyes. 'Her eyesight started to fail and so... I used to help her out.'

She reached behind to support herself against a shelf. Of course he would love their baby. How could she have doubted it? A man who took the time to help an elderly lady sew because that was what she loved to do...because he loved her...

She swallowed and blinked hard. 'You'd make curtains for me?'

'Sure I will.' He suddenly frowned. 'Do you have a sewing machine?'

'My grandmother's will be rattling around somewhere.'

He shrugged again. 'Then no problem.'

Her eyes filled. He backed up a step, rubbed a fist across his mouth. 'Uh, Marianna...you're not going to cry, are you?'

She fanned her eyes. 'Pregnancy hormones,' she whispered.

He moved in close and took her shoulders in

his hands. 'Okay, remember the drill. Close your eyes and take a deep breath.' As he counted to six she pulled in a long, slow breath. 'Hold.' She held. 'Now let it out to the count of six.'

They repeated that three times. When they were finished and she'd opened her eyes, he stepped back, letting his hands drop to his sides. 'Better?'

'Yes, thank you.'

'It's the silliest things, isn't it, that set you off?'

'Uh-huh.'

He snorted. 'It's just a pair of curtains.'

Oh, no, it wasn't. She spun around and pretended to consider the other rolls of fabric arrayed in front of them. These weren't just curtains. They were proof of his commitment to their baby. That wasn't nothing. It was huge…and she had to remember moments like this when he turned all cold and distant and unreadable. He was here for the baby. And he was here for her.

Who was there for him?

She swung back to him. 'You've been incredibly patient with me, Ryan. You haven't hassled me once yet about keeping up my end of our bargain.'

'You haven't been feeling well. Plus you've been working hard on the estate. I've no desire to add to your stress levels.'

He might be cool and controlled but he had a kind heart. 'I've done enough mooching and mood swinging.' From here on in she meant to help him as much as he helped her. 'I need to make another stop before we call it a day.'

'No problem.'

She couldn't help it. She reached up on tiptoe and kissed him.

CHAPTER SIX

'YOU SAID YOU wanted to learn about babies, right?'

Ryan eased back from where he taped the kitchen windows, to find Marianna setting a pile of bags onto the dining table. His pulse rate kicked up a notch, though he couldn't explain why. 'That's right.' He *needed* to learn about babies if he had any hope of making a halfway decent father.

She sent him a smile that carried the same warmth as the lavender-scented air drifting in from the French doors. It reminded him of how she'd smiled at him yesterday when he'd told her he'd make those stupid curtains she wanted.

It reminded him of the way she'd *kissed* him yesterday.

And just like that his skin tightened and he had to fight the rush of blood through his body—a rush that urged him to recklessness. He ground his teeth against it. Recklessness would wreck everything.

Marianna hadn't kissed him as a come-on or an invitation. She'd reached up on tiptoe and had pressed her warm, laughing lips to his in a moment of gratitude and high spirits. It wasn't the kind of kiss that should rock a man's world. It wasn't the kind of kiss that should keep a man up all night.

And yet hunger, need and desire had been gnawing away at him with a cruel persistence ever since. And now Marianna stood there smiling at him, eyes dancing, bouncing as if she could barely contain the energy coursing through her petite frame, and it was all he could do to bite back a groan.

Her smile wavered and she bit her lip. 'You don't have other plans do you? Earlier you said you didn't mean to start painting in here until tomorrow.'

He wanted the smile back on her face. 'No plans.' Today he was prepping the walls for painting…and then getting to work on that report. He set the roll of tape to the kitchen bench and moved straight over to the table. 'I don't want the paint fumes making you feel sick. I thought that if I paint while you're at work…'

'The worst of it will have passed?' She wrinkled her nose—her darn gorgeous nose.

Don't notice her nose. Don't notice her mouth. Don't notice anything below her neck!

He shoved his hands into the pockets of his jeans. 'I'll air the house as well as I can. I bought an extractor fan, so…' He held out crossed fingers before shoving his hand into his pocket again where it was firmly out of temptation's way.

'Have I said thank you yet?'

Dear God in heaven, he couldn't risk her kissing him again. 'You have.' To distract her from further displays of gratitude, he nodded towards the bags. 'What have you got there?'

'A lesson.'

He tried to pull his mind to the task in hand. *Pay attention.* He had to learn how to take care of a baby.

She reached into the nearest bag and, with a flourish, pulled out a…

He blinked and backed up a step. "Uh, Marianna, that's a doll.' He scratched the back of his neck and glared at her from beneath a lock of hair that had fallen forward on his forehead. He really should get it cut. 'Don't you think we're a little old to be playing with dolls?'

She stared at that lock of hair and for a tension-fraught moment he thought she meant to lean across and push it out of his eyes. Hastily, he ran a hand back through his hair himself. She blinked and then shook herself. He let out a breath, his heart thumping.

She, however, seemed completely oblivious to his state. She dangled the doll—a life-sized version from what he could make out—from its foot, and smirked at him. 'Ooh, is the big strong man frightened of the itty-bitty dolly?'

He scowled. 'Don't be ridiculous.'

A laugh bubbled out of her and she sashayed around the table still dangling that stupid doll by its foot. 'Is your super-duper masculinity threatened by a little dolly?'

He snaked a hand around her head and drew her face in close to his. 'Tread carefully, Marianna.'

Her curls, all silk and sass, tickled his hand. 'I'm holding on by a thread here. My so-called masculinity is telling me to throw caution to the wind. It's telling me to kiss you, to take you to my bed and make love with you until you can barely stand.' And then he told her in the most straightforward, vivid language at his command exactly what he craved to do.

Her eyes darkened until they were nearly black. Her lips parted and she stared at his mouth as if she were parched. The pulse in her throat pounded. If he touched his lips to that spot they'd both be lost.

He hauled in a breath. With a super-human effort he let her go. She made a tiny sound halfway between an outbreath and a whimper that arrowed straight to his groin. He closed his eyes and gritted his teeth. 'You told me that if I do that—here in your real world—that I will hurt you, break your heart. I don't want to do that.'

He cracked open his eyes to find her nodding and smoothing a hand across her chest. She gripped the doll by its leg as if it were a hammer. He reached out and plucked it from her. 'There's no need to hurt poor dolly, though, is there?'

He said it to make her smile. It didn't work. She moved back around the other side of the table, her movements jerky and uncoordinated. It hurt him somehow. It hurt to think he'd caused her even momentarily to lose her natural grace and bounce. Her gaze darted to him and away again. 'I'm sorry. I didn't mean for that to come across as any kind of…teasing.'

'I know. It's just…I'm…' He was teetering. He bit back a curse. 'I shouldn't have said anything. I—'

'No, no! It's best that I know.'

Not if it made her feel awkward. He shoved his hands as deep into his pockets as he could. 'It will pass, you know?'

'Oh, I know.' She nodded vigorously. 'It always does.'

He frowned then, recalling her brothers' taunting, *Paulo*. 'That sounds like the voice of experience.'

Her head snapped up. 'So what if it is?'

He blinked, but he had to admit that she had a point.

'It's okay for you to feel that way, but not me? It's okay for you to have had a lot of lovers, but not for me?'

'Not what I meant,' he growled. 'But if you do have experience in this…area, maybe you can hand out a tip or two about how to make it pass quickly.'

'Oh.' Her shoulders sagged. She lifted her hands and let them drop. 'In the past I haven't always had what's considered a good…attention span where men are concerned. I meet a new guy and it's all exciting and fun for a couple of weeks and then…'

Curiosity inched through him. 'And then?'

She wrinkled that cute nose. 'I don't know. It becomes dull, a bit boring and tedious.'

'This happens to you a lot?'

She shrugged, not meeting his eye.

'Which is why your brothers came up with the Paulo moniker.'

Her chin lifted. 'I believe in true love, okay? I don't believe there's anything wrong with looking for it.' Her chin hitched up higher. 'And I don't believe one should settle for anything less.'

'So... When a guy doesn't come up to scratch you what—dump him?'

She glared at him. 'What am I supposed to do? String him along and let him think I'm in love with him?'

'Of course not! I just—'

'I'd hate for any man to do that to me.' She folded her arms. 'I don't believe anyone should settle for anything less than true love.'

He couldn't have found a woman more unlike him if he'd tried!

'So what if I have high expectations of the man I mean to spend the rest of my life with? I'm more than happy for him to have high expectations of me too.'

Right...wow. 'So, you're happy to kiss a lot of frogs in this search for your Prince Charming?'

'Just because a man isn't my Prince Charming doesn't make him a frog, Ryan.'

Right.

She glanced at him. 'Isn't it like that for you—

things becoming a bit boring and tedious after a while?'

He shook his head. 'One-night stands, that's what I do. No promises, no complications…and no time for them to become boring.' At her raised eyebrow he shuffled his feet. 'And once in a blue moon I might indulge in a holiday fling. A week is a long-term commitment in my book.'

'I should be flattered,' she said, her lips twisting in a wry humour that had a grin tugging at the corners of his mouth. She pulled out a chair and plonked down on it. 'What a pair.'

Cautiously he eased into the chair opposite.

She brightened, turning to him. 'All you need to do is start boring me.'

'I've been trying that with the colour charts.'

Her face fell. 'But I don't find them boring.' She tapped a finger to her chin. 'I could try nagging you,' she offered.

His lips twitched. A laugh shot out of her. 'Are you calling me a nag?'

'I wouldn't dream of it.'

She slapped her hands to the table, her eyes dancing. 'You're a bore and I'm a nag!'

Laughter spilled from her then—contagious, infectious—and Ryan found his entire body suddenly convulsing with it, every muscle juddering, a rush of warmth shooting through him. Belly-deep roars of laughter blasted out of him and he was helpless to quieten them even when he developed a stitch in his side.

Marianna laughed just as hard, her legs bouncing up and down, her curls dancing and tears that she tried to stem with her palms pouring down her cheeks. Every time he started to get himself back under control, Marianna would let loose with another giggle or snort and they'd both set off shrieking again. It was a complete overreaction, but the release in tension was irresistible.

'What on earth...?' Nico slid into the room, breathing hard. 'It sounds as if someone is being murdered in here!'

An utterance that only made Marianna laugh harder. Ryan choked back another burst of mirth. 'I'm thinking if I told you that I'm a bore and Marianna is a nag, that you wouldn't get the joke.'

'You'd be right.' But Nico's face softened when he glanced at his sister. He said something to her in Italian. She slowly sobered, although she retained an obscenely wide smile, and nodded.

It was stupid to feel excluded, but he did.

Marianna shot upright and clapped her hands.

'Ryan, will the painting be finished in here—' she gestured around the living, dining and kitchen areas '—by Saturday?'

He shrugged. 'Sure.' That was nearly a week away.

'Nico, are you busy next Saturday night? I want to invite you and Angelo for dinner—a house-warming dinner in my new home.'

Nico's face darkened. 'Are you sure you wouldn't prefer to live up at the villa?'

'Positive.' She tossed her glorious head of hair. 'Now say you'll come to dinner.'

He stared at her for a moment longer and finally smiled. 'I'd be delighted to.' He glanced at Ryan. 'I'll bring the wine.'

Ryan had a feeling that was meant to be some kind of subtle set down, but before he could form a response Nico's gaze lit on the doll. His mouth hooked up. *'You're playing dolls with my sister?'*

He squirmed and ran a finger around the collar of his shirt.

'We're learning to change a diaper,' Marianna announced.

Ah, so that had been her plan.

She raced around the table and dragged her brother across to the doll. 'You're going to want to play with *mia topolino* when it is born, yes?'

'Naturally.'

'"*Mia topolino*"?' Ryan asked.

'My little mouse,' she translated for him and his gut clenched. She had a pet name for their baby?

She turned back to Nico. 'You're going to want to babysit, yes?'

'Of course.'

'Then you need to know how to change a diaper.'

'I can already do so.'

Ryan stared at the other man. He could?

Marianna, however, refused to take Nico at his word. She shoved the doll at him and then reached into another bag and brandished a disposable nappy. Ryan had never seen one before. With a supreme lack of self-consciousness, Nico quickly and deftly placed said nappy on the baby...uh, doll. Ryan frowned. That didn't look too hard.

He caught the doll when Nico tossed it to him with a mocking, 'Your turn.'

His stomach screwed up tight, but he refused to back down from the challenge. How hard could it be? He held out a hand to Marianna like a doctor waiting for a scalpel. 'Nappy.' She blinked. 'Diaper,' he amended. 'We call them nappies in Australia.'

She passed one across to him. He stared at it,

turned it over. Why didn't these things come with Front and Back labels? And instructions? Gingerly he rested the baby on the table. *Doll, not baby.*

Nico's hands rested on his hips. 'You need to keep a hand on the baby to make sure it doesn't roll off the table.'

Marianna shushed her brother. Ryan tried to keep hold of the doll with one hand while unfolding the nappy with the other. Nico snickered. Damn it! He was all thumbs.

Ryan blocked his audience out as he tried to decipher the puzzle in front of him. Slipping what he hoped was the rear of the nappy beneath the baby, he brought the front up, and secured the sticky tabs at the sides. There, that hadn't been too hard, and for a first attempt it didn't look too bad. He lifted the baby under the arms prepared to crow at his performance, but the nappy slid off and fell to the floor with a soft thud. Damn!

Nico snorted. 'And you call yourself a father?'

Marianna opened her mouth, her eyes flashing, but Ryan touched her arm and she closed it again. He glared at Nico. 'I call myself a father-to-be.' He tossed the doll back. 'Show me how you did it again.' He would master this!

Twenty minutes later Ryan finally lifted the doll

and this time his effort at least stayed in place. Discarded diapers littered the table and the floor. He shook the doll.

'You're not—'

Ryan held up a finger to the man opposite. 'I know you're not supposed to shake babies, but this is a doll, in case you hadn't noticed. I've already killed it multiple times by letting it roll off the table, smothering it beneath a sea of nappies, and it's probably concussed from where I accidentally cracked its head on the back of the chair.'

Thank heavens Marianna had the foresight to give him a doll to practise on.

'I know it's probably peed on me—' that discussion had proved particularly enlightening '—puked on me and probably bitten me, but...' he shook the doll again '...that nappy isn't going anywhere.'

He felt a ludicrous sense of achievement. He could change a nappy!

'Don't get too cocky. Wait until you have to change a dirty diaper. One that smells so bad it's like a kick in the gut and—'

'Enough, Nico,' Marianna said. 'My turn now.'

She took the doll, and, with her tongue caught between her teeth, repeated the process of putting the diaper on. Ryan moved in closer to check her handiwork. 'That looks pretty good.'

She shook her head and frowned. 'I did what you did. I didn't make it tight enough.' She slid several fingers between the diaper and the doll to prove her point. 'It's just… I don't want to cut the poor baby's circulation off.' She glanced across at her brother. 'Are you going to say something cutting about my prospective mothering abilities?'

Nico shuffled his feet and glowered at the floor. 'Of course not.'

A surge of affection swamped Ryan then. She'd just risked criticism and scorn from her brother to show solidarity with him. Nobody had done anything like that for him before, and he was fairly certain he didn't deserve it now, but…to not feel cut off, adrift, alone. To feel connected and part of a team, it was… He rolled his shoulders. It was kind of nice.

Nico pointed a finger at Marianna. 'You've changed diapers before. You must have at harvest time. We have so many workers then. Many of them with children,' he added for Ryan's benefit.

'I did, but I was never particularly good at it and…well, people stopped asking me.' Her shoulders had started inching up towards her ears. In the next moment she tossed her head. 'I was really good at keeping the children entertained, cajoling them out of tears and bad tempers.'

For the first time it struck him that Marianna might be feeling as intimidated and overwhelmed as he did about their impending parenthood.

'And what's more, dearest brother of mine, if you mean to continue standing there criticising us, then be warned that I'll tell Ryan how you used to play Barbie dolls with me when I was a little girl.'

Nico backed up a step and pointed behind him. 'I'll, uh, leave you to it. I have work to do.' He turned and fled.

Ryan stared after him. Had he really played dolls with his little sister? He glanced at Marianna, who was having a second attempt at getting the nappy on, and then at the door again. The guy couldn't be all bad.

'Ryan?'

He turned to face her more fully. 'Yes?'

'I'm sorry about my brother.'

'No apology needed. And thank you.' He gestured to the table, the doll and the pile of nappies. 'This was a great idea. I'm going to have to start practising.' He was going to be the best damn nappy changer the Amatucci clan had ever seen.

* * *

Marianna watched Ryan put, oh, yet another diaper on the doll, his face a mask of determination, and something inside her softened. He was trying so hard. 'You're getting better,' she offered.

'We're going to run out of diapers soon.'

It was sweet too that he called them diapers now, probably for her benefit. 'We can get more.'

He glanced at her; his eyes danced for a moment, bringing out the deep blue in their depths that so intrigued her. 'I'll make a deal with you, Mari...'

The easy shortening of her name and the familiarity it implied made her break out in delicious gooseflesh. *It's a lie—an illusion.* She couldn't forget that. 'A deal?'

'I'll be the main diaper changer if you take on the role of dealing with Junior's tears and temper.'

'We'd need to be co-parenting together full-time for that kind of deal to work.' It was starting to hit her how difficult single parenthood was going to be. Sure, Ryan wanted to be involved, but they both knew the bulk of the baby's care would fall to her.

Unless Ryan moved to Monte Calanetti and they agreed to a fifty-fifty child custody arrangement. She bit her lip. She didn't like that thought. She wanted the baby with her full-time. She rolled her lip between her teeth. Okay, she was honest enough to admit that she might want the occasional night off, but nothing more. She didn't want the baby spending half its time away from her. She glanced at Ryan to find he'd gone deathly pale. What on earth…?

She went back over their conversation and then rolled her eyes. 'Get over yourself! I'm not angling for a marriage proposal. We decided against that, remember?'

He searched her face, and slowly his colour returned. He nodded and dragged a hand down his face.

'I haven't forgotten. You're commitment-shy and a lone wolf.'

'While you have a short attention span when it comes to men.'

She folded her arms and stared at him for a long moment. 'You're different from the other men I've known, though. This is different—us…we're different.' Why was that? 'But it doesn't mean I want to marry you.' She couldn't fool herself that it meant anything or that it would lead anywhere. 'I've never stayed friends with any of my previous lovers.' That probably had something to do with it.

'Me neither.'

'And I've certainly never had a baby with anyone before.'

He raised both hands. 'Nor I.'

'So obviously this is going to be different from any other experience we've had before, right?'

'Absolutely.'

She glanced at him but it wasn't relief that trickled through her. The itch she couldn't reach, the one right in the middle of her back between her shoulder blades, pricked with a renewed ferocity that made her grit her teeth. Her skin prickled, her stomach clenched, and a roaring hunger bellowed through her with so much ferocity it was all she could do not to scream. Sleeping with Ryan would sate that itch and need, soothe the burn and bite. Sleeping with Ryan would quieten the fears racing through her and—

'Don't look at me like that, Marianna!'

She started, the hunger in his eyes making her sway towards him, but he shook his head and took a step back. Instinct told her that if she continued to stare at him so boldly, so…lustfully, he'd seize her in his arms, kiss her and they probably wouldn't even make it to her bedroom.

She craved that like a drug. She craved it more

than she'd ever craved anything. To fall into Ryan's arms and lose herself in a world of sensation and physical gratification, what a dream! But… What she felt for Ryan was different from what she'd felt for anyone. The intensity of it frightened her. She didn't want this man breaking her heart. That'd be a disaster. Through their child, they'd be tied to each other for the rest of their lives. It'd leave her no room to get over him.

She gripped the back of a chair and dragged her gaze from his. Pulling the chair out, she fell into it. 'I really, *really* can't wait for the time when you become boring. I…I have things to do.' With that she leapt up and strode away, and all the while her fickle heart urged her to turn back and throw herself into Ryan's arms, to throw caution to the wind.

Ryan pounced on his phone the moment it rang. 'Ryan White.'

'It's confirmed. Conti Industries are getting cold feet,' his assistant in Rome said without preamble. She knew his impatience with small talk and had learned long ago to get straight to the point. Time was money.

'Why?' Was someone conducting a smear campaign, attempting to discredit him?

'It appears the fact that you're not personally in Rome at the moment has them questioning your commitment.'

Damn it! He wheeled away, raking a hand back through his hair. He'd been afraid this would happen—that Conti Industries would develop cold feet. Why on earth had he promised to stay in Monte Calanetti for a whole month? He needed his head read!

He straightened, moving immediately into damage control. 'Can you arrange a meeting?'

'I already have.'

He let out a breath. 'That's the reason I pay you the big bucks.' Face-to-face with the Conti Industries' executive committee he'd be able to turn things around, prove their former faith in him wasn't a mistake.

'But it's this afternoon. You need to get down here *pronto*.'

Today!

'I tried making it for tomorrow, but they insisted. They're viewing this meeting as, quote, "a validation of your commitment to their project and your ability to deliver". They've left me in no doubt that agreeing to meet is an unprecedented demonstration of faith. I don't need to tell you what'll happen if you miss this meeting.'

He pressed his lips together. No, she didn't. If he weren't in Rome this afternoon, the whole deal would go down the gurgler. He thrust out his jaw. He wasn't letting that happen. Not without a fight.

'I'll be there,' he said, bringing the call to an abrupt end.

He glanced through his electronic diary as he hauled on a suit. The only thing he had slotted in was Marianna's information session this evening. He let out a breath. He'd be able to catch up on that another time. He slipped a tie around his collar and tied a perfect Windsor knot. He'd ring her later to let her know he couldn't make it.

As he drove away from the vineyard a short time later the rush of chasing the big deal sped through him, filling him with adrenaline and fire. He'd missed that cut-and-thrust this past week. This was the world where he belonged, not decorating nurseries. Drumming his fingers against the car's steering wheel, he wondered if he could cut his time at Marianna's vineyard a week or two short.

Marianna glanced at her watch and paced the length of her living room before whirling back. It

was ten past six. Where was Ryan? The information session at the clinic started in twenty minutes!

She'd reminded him about it this morning. He'd
told her he hadn't forgotten, that it was in his diary,
that he'd drive them. So where was he?

She glanced at her watch again. Eleven minutes past six. With a growl, she dialled his mobile
number and pressed her phone to her ear. It went
straight to voicemail. Brilliant. 'Where are you?
The session starts in nineteen minutes! I can't wait
any longer. I'll meet you at the clinic.'

Seizing her car keys, she stormed out and drove
herself to the town's medical clinic. She'd just
parked when her phone buzzed in her handbag. A
text. From Ryan.

Something came up. In Rome. Won't be back till
tomorrow. Sorry, couldn't be helped. Meeting
very important. Will make next info session.

He couldn't even be bothered to ring her?

She stared at the screen. Blinking hard, she
shoved the phone back into her bag. Right, well, she
knew exactly where she and the baby stood in the
list of Ryan's priorities—right at the very bottom.

How on earth did either one of them think this
was going to work?

* * *

'Don't even think about it!'

Marianna spun around, clutching her chest, to find Ryan—with hands on his hips—silhouetted in the large cellar door. As he was backlit by the sun she couldn't see his face, but she had a fair inkling that he was glaring at her. She gestured to the barrel, her heart pounding. 'It's empty.'

He moved forward and effortlessly lifted it onto her trolley.

She swallowed and tried to smile. 'See? Not heavy.'

He stabbed a finger at her. 'You shouldn't be lifting anything. You should be looking after yourself.'

She batted his finger away. 'Stop being such a mother hen. I'm used to this kind of manual labour. It won't hurt the baby.'

'But why take the risk?' He gestured to the barrel. 'You must have staff here who can take care of these things for you?'

Of course they did, but she didn't want anyone thinking she couldn't do her job. She didn't want anyone thinking she was using her pregnancy as an excuse to slacken off. She wanted everyone to see how steady and professional she'd become since returning from Australia. She wanted everyone to see how she'd developed her potential, wanted them to say what a talent she was, what an asset for Vigneto Calanetti.

'I don't want to lose my fitness or my strength, Ryan. I'll need them for when I return to work after my maternity leave.'

He blinked.

'I'm going to need both for the labour too.' The information evening had brought that home to her with stunning—and awful—clarity. The information evening he *hadn't* attended so what right did he think he had ordering her around like this now?

He frowned. 'You're active—always on the go. I don't think you need to worry on that head.'

Ha! If he, Nico and Angelo had any say in the matter she wouldn't lift a finger for the next six and a half months. Well, at dinner on Saturday night she'd show her brothers how accomplished and capable she'd become. She'd wow them with her new house, a superb dinner and marvellous conversation. They'd realise she was a woman in charge of her own destiny—they'd stop worrying she'd screwed up her life and…and they'd all move forward from there.

'Are you worried about the labour?'

'Not a bit of it,' she lied. She straightened. 'How was your meeting in Rome?'

'Yes, I'm so sorry about that. It really couldn't be helped.'

Why wasn't he asking about the info session? She tried to keep the disapproving tone out of her voice. 'Did you come looking especially for me? Was there something you needed?'

'Just a break from painting for a bit.' He grimaced. 'The smell can become a little overwhelming.'

'I'm sorry. I didn't think about—'

'I'm enjoying it. Don't apologise. It's just…I found myself curious about what you do all day and—' he gestured around '—this place.'

So he was interested in her work, but not their baby. She had to remind herself that the idea of a baby was still very new to him, and that at least he was trying. And she couldn't wholly blame him—to her mind vineyards and wineries were fascinating.

He rolled his shoulders. 'I mean, you leave at the crack of dawn each day.'

She suddenly laughed. 'Ryan, I'm not leaving early to avoid you. I've always been a lark and I love checking the vines in the early morning when everything is fresh and drenched in dew. It means I can have the afternoons free if I want.' At his look she added, 'At the moment there's a certain amount of work that needs to be done, but it doesn't really matter when I do it.'

'The convenience of being your own boss.'

'Don't you believe it. Nico is the boss here. Don't let his easy-going mildness fool you. He has a killer work ethic.'

'Easy-going?' he choked. 'Mild?'

She laughed at his disbelief and led him out of the door and gestured to the row upon row of vines marching up the hill, all starting to flower. Those flowers might not be considered pretty, but she thought them beautiful. And if each of them were properly pollinated they'd become a glorious luscious grape. 'Beautiful, isn't it?'

He blew out a long breath and nodded.

'I can offer our child a good home, Ryan. A good life.'

'I know that.'

She hoped he did. 'Would you like a tour of our facilities here?'

'I'd love that.' He suddenly frowned. 'But only because I'm curious, not because I doubt you.'

She wasn't so convinced, but she showed him

everything. She showed him what she looked for in a grape and what she was working towards. She took him to see the presses, the fermentation vats and the aging vessels. She even took him into the bottling room. She ended the tour at the cellar door where she had him try several of their more renowned wines.

'Things are relatively quiet at the moment, but at harvest time it becomes crazy here. In September, we eat, breathe and sleep grapes.' She glanced up at him. 'You should try and make it back then to experience it. It's frenetic but fun.'

'I'll see what I can do.' But he already knew he'd be tied up working the Conti contract. He glanced beyond her and nodded. 'Nico.'

She turned to find Nico with their new neighbour Louisa standing behind her. She straightened, hoping Nico didn't think she was skiving off. 'I was just showing Ryan around. Hello, Louisa.'

The other woman smiled and it somehow helped to ease the tension between the two men. 'I understand congratulations are in order,' the other woman said. 'News of your pregnancy has spread like wildfire through the village.'

She could barely contain her grin. *A baby!* 'Thank you.' Beside her, Ryan shifted and she came back to herself. 'Louisa, this is Ryan White. He's staying with me for a bit. Ryan, this is Louisa Harrison. She recently inherited the vineyard and glorious *palazzo* next door. Speaking of which, how are the renovations coming along?'

Louisa lifted a shoulder. 'No sooner did the architect arrive than it seemed the renovations to the chapel started. There are workers swarming all over the *palazzo*! The schedule is to have it completed by the end of July. But…it's such a big job.'

Marianna nodded. The *palazzo* was glorious and the family chapel absolutely exquisite, but it'd been neglected for a long time. It'd be wonderful to see it restored to its former glory.

'The architect is based in Rome and has a very good reputation,' Louisa continued. 'He used to holiday here as a child apparently. It seemed sensible to choose a firm that had connections to the area.'

'What's his name?' Marianna asked.

'Logan Cascini.'

'I remember him! He and Angelo were a similar age, I think. I'm sure they hung out together.'

Nico nodded. 'They did.'

'It'll be lovely to see him again. Is he married?' Was there a new woman in town who needed befriending? 'Any *bambinos*?' She bit back a smile. It wasn't as if she had babies on the brain or anything.

Louisa shook her head.

Beside her, Ryan shifted again and she glanced up at him, puzzled at the sudden tension that coursed through him. He glared at Nico. 'While you're here, perhaps you can talk some sense into your sister and tell her heavy lifting is off the agenda until after the baby is born.'

Oh, brilliant. She and Nico had already had words on this head.

Nico stiffened. 'Marianna?'

'I caught her lifting a barrel.'

She sent Ryan an exasperated glare. The big fat tale teller! 'It was an *empty* barrel.'

Nico let forth with a torrent of Italian curses that made her wince. Finally he stabbed a finger at her. 'Why can you not get this through your thick skull?'

She started to shrivel inside.

'No more lifting. One more time, Mari, and I'm firing you!'

Her jaw dropped. 'You can't!' This was her job, her work, her home!

'I can and I will!'

He would too. She battled the lump in her throat.

'No more lifting! You hear me?'

All she could manage was a nod. *Screw-up. Useless. Failure.* The accusations went around and around in her head. So much for proving her worth.

'Why have you not been keeping a better eye on her?' Nico shot at Ryan.

'Me? You're her employer!'

She closed her eyes. She opened them again when Louisa touched her arm. 'How have you been feeling? Have you had much morning sickness?'

She could've hugged her for changing the subject and bringing Ryan and Nico's finger-pointing to a halt. 'A little. And the morning part of that is a lie. It can happen at any time of the day.' She sucked her bottom lip into her mouth. 'I probably shouldn't have announced my pregnancy until after my scan.' What if something went wrong? Everybody would know and—

'But you were excited.'

Louisa smiled her understanding, and it helped Marianna to straighten and push her shoulders back. This incident might've been a backward step as far as Nico's view of her went, but she was going to be a mother, and she was determined to be a good one.

'Speaking of which,' Nico said, 'I believe you said your scan is tomorrow, yes?'

Ryan stiffened and then swung to her. 'Tomorrow?'

Nico's eyes narrowed and she could see his view of her maturity take another nosedive. *Damn it!*

She waved an airy hand in the air. 'Don't tell me you've forgotten? You did say you'd take me.'

To Ryan's credit, he adjusted swiftly and smoothly. 'Of course. Just as we planned.'

Damn it again! She hadn't wanted him to take her. What use would she have for a man who had no interest in hearing his baby's heartbeat?

CHAPTER SEVEN

MARIANNA THREW HERSELF down on a bench in the garden, slapping a palm to her forehead. 'Well done, you…doofus!' she muttered. To think she'd been making progress where Angelo and Nico were concerned, to think—

She leaned to the side until her head rested on the arm of the bench and did what she could to halt the flood of recriminations pounding through her. She tried the breathing technique that Ryan had taught her, but in this instance it didn't work. All it did was bring to mind the light in his eyes when he'd returned to the cottage to paint her walls. It'd told her that the subject of her scan—of her not telling him the actual date of said scan—would be the topic of conversation the moment she returned.

Yay. More talking. Which, of course, was why she was hiding out in the garden like a coward.

Very adult of you, Marianna.

Heat pricked the backs of her eyes and a lump swelled in her throat. What if they were right?

What if she were making a hash of everything? She pressed a hand to her stomach. What if she made a mess of her baby's life?

'It's all a mess!'

For a moment she thought Nico's voice sounded in her own mind. When Louisa answered with, 'What do you mean?' Marianna realised that her brother and their neighbour passed close by on the other side of the hedge. The hedge's shade and its new spring growth shielded her from view. She shrank back against the bench, not wanting Nico to see her so upset.

'I don't trust this latest man of Marianna's.'

Marianna wanted to cover her ears. Ryan wasn't hers.

'Can I give you a word of advice, Nico?'

Her brother must've nodded because Louisa continued. 'You don't have to like Ryan, but if Marianna has decided that he's to be a part of her baby's life, then you're going to have to accept that. He's going to be a part of your niece or nephew's life for evermore—in effect, a part of your extended family. You don't have to like him, but if Marianna has asked that you respect her decision, then you're going to have to find a way to get along with him... for both Marianna and the baby's sake.'

'But—'

'No buts, Nico. You know, if you eased up on him for a bit, you might even find yourself liking Ryan.'

Her brother snorted. 'You think?'

'You never know.'

Marianna remained where she was, barely moving, until the voices drifted out of earshot. She hadn't meant to overhear. She hadn't meant to throw everyone into chaos with her baby news either. She forced herself off the bench and set off for the cottage.

The smell of paint hit her the moment she entered. She paused on the threshold, but her stomach remained calm and quiet and with a relieved breath she continued down the hallway to the living area.

She pulled to an immediate halt with a delighted, 'Oh!' Clutching her hands beneath her chin, she gazed around in wonder at the transformation a coat of deliciously tranquil 'sea foam'-coloured paint had created. Ryan must've worked his socks off!

She completed a slow circle. 'Oh, Ryan, it's perfect. Thank you.' She ached to lie on the sofa and revel in the calm, draw it into her soul.

'You weren't going to tell me that your appointment is tomorrow, were you?'

She bit back a sigh. The calm was only an illusion. In the same way her and Ryan's *friendship* was an illusion. She turned towards the dining table where he sat. He rose and she wished herself back outside in her shady glen. 'Tea?' She stumbled into the kitchen and filled the kettle.

'Marianna?'

She didn't like the growl in his voice or the latent possessiveness rippling beneath it. 'No.' She turned and faced him, hands on her hips. 'You have that correct. I wasn't going to tell you about tomorrow's appointment.'

'Why not?'

She pulled two cups towards her and tossed teabags into them. 'Because you have no interest in being there.' Just as he'd had no interest in attending the information session.

'I said I would drive you.'

'And I told you I don't need a taxi service!'

His head reared back as if she'd slapped him. 'But…we're a team.'

Were they? Wasn't that just a polite fiction? 'If you don't want to be present at the scan, Ryan, then you're more use to me here fixing up the cottage.'

She spoke as baldly and bluntly as she could to remind herself that what they had here was a deal, an arrangement, and not a relationship.

He dragged a hand across his jaw, his eyes troubled. 'Then why the pretence in front of Nico?'

She pulled in a breath, held it to the count of three and let it out again. 'Because I don't want him to think badly of you…and I don't want him to think badly of me.'

'Why would he think badly of you? He worships the ground you walk on.'

She snorted and he frowned. She swung away to pour boiling water into their mugs. 'I'm his pesky little sister who's always getting into scrapes.'

'He adores you, Mari. He'd die for you.'

'I know.' He spoke nothing less than the truth.

'So would Angelo.'

That was the truth too. But sometimes she felt the weight of their love would suffocate her.

She started. 'Oh! I made you a chamomile tea. Should I—?'

'You should've asked me to make the tea! You've been on your feet all day.'

She nodded at the walls. 'And you haven't?' Not only was he painting her house, he was working on some new company report or other, taking endless calls on his mobile phone and making video calls on his laptop. If anyone were the slacker around here it'd be her.

He came around and took the mug from her. 'This will be fine, thank you.' When he gestured for her to take a seat on the sofa, she submitted. If they had to *talk*, then they might as well be comfortable while they did so.

'Look, I know you love your brothers.' He sat in the armchair opposite. 'I know you would die for them too.'

She would. In a heartbeat. She blinked, frowned. Did her love ever suffocate them?

'I understand it's important to you that I get along with them.'

He took a sip of his tea and grimaced.

She couldn't help grimacing too. In sympathy. 'You don't have to drink that, you know? Chamomile is an acquired taste.'

'You went to the trouble of making it, therefore I mean to drink it.'

What an enigma this man was proving to be. She slumped back. 'Getting on with my brothers isn't entirely in your control, Ryan. It's up to them too.'

His eyes had turned a stormy green that she was

starting to recognise as a mixture of confusion and frustration. 'The fact you lied to Nico—'

'Lied is a bit harsh!'

'Well, let him believe I was included in tomorrow's appointment, then.'

Not that it'd worked. Nico had seen through her deception.

'Leads me to believe,' Ryan continued, 'that being present at this scan is something a *good* father would do.'

She leapt to her feet, setting her mug to the coffee table before she could spill it. 'Oh! You think?' How could this man be so clueless?

No, no, he couldn't be this clueless. It was just that whole stupid lone-wolf thing he had going and—

'Oh!' She stopped dead before racing across to the kitchen again. 'You made the kitchen curtains.' She ran her hands down the material. How had she not noticed them earlier? 'They're…*exactly* what I wanted.' They would look wonderful against the vibrant yellow of the walls once Ryan had painted in here—a nook of colour amidst the calm.

His voice came from behind her. 'You like them?'

She loved them. A lump blocked her throat and all she could do was nod. They were perfect. She glanced around the cottage at the new paint on the living and dining room walls, the kitchen primed and ready for its first coat of paint tomorrow, and at those darn curtains. Ryan was doing everything she asked of him without a murmur of complaint. He was doing everything he could to help her create the perfect home for their baby.

She moved across to the dining table and picked up the doll lying there—a doll sporting a perfect diaper and a ridiculous smile. She clutched the doll to her chest and swung to face him. 'Ryan, how can you not want to see the first pictures of our baby? How can you not want to hear its heartbeat?'

He dragged a hand across his jaw, not meeting her gaze. 'I have work to do.'

She dropped the doll back to the table. 'Work that's more important than your own child?'

Tension shot through him. With an oath, he started to pace. 'The truth?' he shot at her.

'The truth,' she demanded.

'Fine, then!' He swung back. 'Attending the ultrasound with you seems...'

'Seems what?' she pushed.

He skewered her to the spot with the ruthless light in his eyes. 'Too intimate.'

She rocked back on her heels, his words shocking her. 'It's not as intimate as the deed that's led us to this point in time.'

'True.' He nodded, his gaze not softening. 'But making love with you—our holiday fling…absolutely nothing out of character for me there.'

Except it'd lasted for a whole week rather than a single night. She left that observation unsaid.

'Attending an ultrasound with a woman…now that's utterly out of character. Can't see what use I'm going to be to you in that scenario, Marianna.'

Her chest cramped up so tight it became an effort to even breathe. Finally she managed a curt nod. 'If you want to become a halfway decent father, Ryan, you're going to have to get over this kind of squeamishness.'

His eyes bugged. 'Squeamishness?'

'Squeamishness about doing family things, feeling able to step up to the plate for another person, being relied upon.'

He swung away. 'I'm supposed to be in Rome tomorrow afternoon.'

'And just for the record, this isn't about you stepping up to the plate for me. It's not about you—' how had he put it? '—being of any use to me. This isn't about you and me.' There was no him and her. 'This is about you and the baby.'

His mouth thinned. 'This is all because I missed that damn info session, isn't it?'

"It's becoming obvious that your work is more important to you than our baby."

"Correction. That particular meeting was more important than attending an info session I can catch again at another time."

"And in the years to come a different important meeting will have you missing your child's second birthday, others will have you missing the school concert, a soccer grand final. You'll cancel promised outings and holidays because something important has come up at work. I want more than that for my child, Ryan. And you should too."

They stared at each other, both breathing hard. She swallowed and shrugged. 'The ultrasound is early—nine-thirty a.m.' He could attend the scan and still make an afternoon appointment in Rome. 'I'm driving myself. If you wish to attend, a flyer for the clinic with its address is on the fridge. I don't want to discuss this any more. I'm tired and I don't feel like fighting.' With that she walked back over to the sofa and picked up her chamomile tea.

He was quiet for a moment. 'I didn't mean to upset you.'

She waved that away.

He strode back and threw himself down into his chair. He leaned towards her suddenly, frowning. 'Are you worried about tomorrow's scan?'

She stared down into her tea. 'Of course not,' she lied.

But… What if she'd somehow hurt their baby? Her fingers tightened about her mug. For the best part of two months she hadn't even realised she was pregnant. She'd been drinking wine and coffee— not copious amounts, but still… She should've been taking special vitamins. If she'd planned this baby, she wouldn't have these worries. She'd have done everything right from the start.

She swallowed. She might be an irresponsible fool and if the scan showed a problem tomorrow she'd have nobody to blame but herself. And now she wouldn't even have the comfort of Ryan's hand to cling to.

Marianna readied herself for the sensation of cold gel on her tummy when the technician's assistant tapped on the door and then popped her head around the curtain that screened Marianna. 'Sorry to disturb, but there's a Mr White out here who claims he's the baby's father.'

Marianna couldn't help it, her heart leapt.

'Shall I send him in?'

Marianna nodded. 'Yes, please.'

A moment later Ryan hovered awkwardly on the other side of the curtain, his face appearing in the gap. 'Sorry, I'm late.'

Marianna ached to hold her hand out to him, but she resisted the urge. She had no intention of making this all seem too *intimate*. 'I wasn't sure you'd make it.' She gestured to the equipment. 'Come on over and watch the show.'

He moved to stand beside her, but he didn't take her hand.

Marianna tried to ignore his warmth and scent, focusing on the monitor as the radiologist moved the sensor across her stomach and pointed out the baby's arms and legs, feet and fingers. She pronounced the baby to be in the best of health and Marianna let out the breath she'd been holding, her eyes still glued to the screen. *Thank you!*

Her heart started to pound, wonder filling her from the inside out, and she couldn't stop from reaching a hand towards the image on the monitor. She couldn't remember a more amazing moment in her life. Her baby!

Their baby.

She turned to Ryan and her heart stilled at the expression that spread across his face. She watched as his amazement turned to awe. He blinked hard several times, and a fist seized her heart. He swallowed and leaned towards the monitor…and she watched him fall in love with their baby.

That was the moment her chest cracked open. She felt as if she were falling and falling—as if there were no end in sight, no bottom to bring her up short—and then Ryan seized her hand, a breath whooshed out of her, and the world righted itself again.

He squeezed her hand, not taking his eyes from the screen. 'That's really something, isn't it?'

'Utterly amazing,' she breathed, not taking her eyes from his face.

But then he suddenly shot back, shaking his fingers free from hers, the colour leaching from him.

'Ryan?'

He glanced at his watch. 'I'm sorry, but if I don't get a move on I won't make my appointment this afternoon in Rome. I won't be back till tomorrow.'

With that he spun on his heel and left the room. Marianna turned back to the monitor and the image of her baby. Her temples started to throb.

Ryan stared around the chaos of the kitchen and grimaced. He rubbed the back of his head. 'What can I do?'

'Nothing!'

He glanced at his watch. Angelo and Nico weren't due to arrive for at least another hour, but…

The house was spick and span with not a single item out of place. Marianna had slaved over it all day. Ryan valued neatness and utility, but this was…*so* neat. Then again, maybe the kitchen made up for it. He turned to view it again and had to blink. The yellow on the walls was…bright.

He spun back to the rest of the room. It wasn't as if the neatness made things sterile, like a hotel room. Marianna's new scatter cushions and strategically draped throw rugs brightened the sofa, making it look like an inviting oasis to rest one's weary bones. But…

He shuffled his feet. 'Marianna—'

'No, no, don't talk to me! I have to concentrate. This recipe is complicated.'

He touched her arm. 'It's just your brothers. They won't care if you ring out for pizza.'

'Ring out?' Her mouth dropped open, her hair fizzing about her face in outrage.

He stared at that mouth and tension coiled up through him.

'I'm not ringing out! This dinner is going to be perfect!'

Why? Not because of him, he hoped. He didn't want her putting this kind of pressure on herself on his behalf.

He tapped a clenched fist against his mouth. It'd be pointless trying to reason with her when she was in this mood, though. Mind you, she'd been distant—wary—ever since he'd returned from Rome yesterday.

He winced anew when he recalled the way he'd bolted from the clinic during the ultrasound. The moment had been... He rubbed his nape. Well, it'd been perfect for a bit...before he'd started to feel as if he were drowning. Emotions he'd had no name for had pummelled him, trying to drag him under, and he'd needed to get away—needed time to breathe and pull himself back together.

It was all of those happy family vibes flying about the room. They'd tried to wrestle him into a straitjacket and put a noose around his neck. Worse still, for a moment he'd wanted to let them.

He didn't do happy families. He'd be the best father he could be to this child, but he wasn't marrying Marianna. He dragged a hand down his face. *That* would be a disaster.

He'd calmed down. Eventually. He had his head together again.

Now all he had to do was get through this evening.

He glanced at Marianna again. Her jerky movements and the way she muttered under her breath told him how much importance she'd placed on this meal. He made a mental note to do all he could to get along with her brothers tonight.

'There's nothing you can do. Go sit on the sofa and enjoy doing nothing for a change.'

He didn't. When she became absorbed again in some complicated manoeuvre involving flour, butter and potato, he slid in behind her and made a start on washing up the tower of dishes that was in danger of toppling over and burying her.

The scent of her earlier preparations—sautéed onion, garlic and bacon—rose up around him, making his mouth water. He managed to clear one entire sink of dishes without her yelling at him to get out from under her feet or accusing him once of being a neat freak. He even managed to dry and put them away, sliding out of her way whenever she spun around to seize another dish or wooden spoon or ingredient.

He was just starting on a second sink full of dishes—how could anyone use so many dishes to make one meal?—when a commotion sounded at the front door and Angelo and Nico marched in.

Angelo carried an armful of flowers in one hand and a gift-wrapped vase under his arm. Nico bore a brightly wrapped gift. 'Happy housewarming!' they bellowed.

Marianna glared at them and pointed to the clock on the wall. 'You're early!'

'We couldn't wait to see you, *bella sorella*,' Angelo said, dropping an arm to her shoulders and easing her away from the stove and towards the living area. In one smooth movement Nico slid into her place and took over the cooking. 'Besides, we come bearing gifts.'

It was masterfully done and if he hadn't had wet hands Ryan would've applauded.

Marianna glanced at the flowers and clasped her hands beneath her chin. 'Oh! They're beautiful.'

Without a word, Ryan took the vase Angelo handed across the breakfast bar and filled it with water.

Marianna spun around to point a finger at Nico. 'I know exactly what the two of you are doing!'

Angelo took the now-filled vase and placed it on the coffee table. 'Should I just dump the flowers in?'

Marianna immediately swung back. 'No, you should not!' And set about arranging the flowers.

'But it doesn't change the fact that I know what the two of you are doing. You still don't think I can cook gnocchi.'

'You can't,' Nico said with a grin. 'And we knew it's what you'd try to make tonight.'

She shrugged. 'It's your favourite.' She straightened. 'And I'll have you know I've become very adept at the dish.'

'No, you haven't,' Angelo said with a grin. 'You're a brilliant tosser of salads, Mari, you make masterful pizzas, and your omelettes are to die for, but gnocchi isn't your thing. In the same way that Nico can't master a good sauterne.'

'Pah!' She waved that away. 'We don't grow the right grapes for sauterne.'

'And yet he keeps trying,' Angelo said with a teasing grin at his brother.

'Ooh, says you.' Marianna rolled her eyes. 'You keep telling me you have a green thumb, but who keeps killing my African violets?'

Ryan watched the three of them tease each other, boss each other, and a chasm of longing suddenly cracked open in his chest. He didn't understand it. He tried to shake it off. He told himself he was glad his child would have this family. And he was…but when Marianna eventually married *the man of her dreams* would their child feel an outsider amidst all of this belonging? As he did.

'You've done a good job in here, Ryan,' Nico said in an undertone. 'How on earth did you make it into the kitchen without having something thrown at you?'

'Subterfuge…and a quick two-step shuffle to get out of her way whenever she was reaching for something.'

Her brothers obviously knew her well. And then it hit him. Nico had just called him Ryan, not Paulo. Did that mean Marianna's brothers had decided on a temporary ceasefire? He put the last dried dish away. 'Anything I can do?'

'Know anything about gnocchi?'

'Nope.'

'Know anything about wine?'

Ryan glanced at the bottle Nico had placed on the bench earlier. 'I know how to pour it.'

'Then pour away.'

He poured three glasses of wine and then filled a fourth with mineral water, three ice cubes and a slice of lime—the exact way Marianna liked it. When he took their drinks to them, though, Marianna pursed her lips, glanced over at Nico, and started to rise. Nico chose that moment to move out from behind the breakfast bar with his glass of wine and handed her the wrapped package, ensuring she remained ensconced on the sofa. 'It's not a housewarming present,' he warned. 'It's a...' He shrugged. 'Open and see.'

Ryan watched in interest, his breath catching in his chest when Marianna pulled forth the most exquisite teddy bear he'd ever seen. Her eyes filled with tears and she hugged it. 'Oh, Angelo and Nico, it's perfect. Just perfect!'

His heart thudded. Why hadn't he thought to buy a toy for their baby? Since the scan all he could think about was the baby—the tiny life growing inside Marianna. The moment he'd been able to make out the baby's image on the monitor a love so powerful and protective had surged through him that, even now, just thinking about it left him reeling. He craved to be the best father he could be. He didn't want this child to doubt for a single second that it was loved.

His hands clenched. Could he really bear to be away from Monte Calanetti once the baby was born? Could he really envisage spending months at a time away from his child?

Nico turned with a wry grin. 'Want to put a diaper on teddy to match the one on dolly?'

He forced a smile to lips that didn't want to work. 'You might be surprised to find yourself with serious competition in the diaper-changing stakes.'

As one, he and Nico turned to Angelo with raised eyebrows. The other man raised his hands. 'No way.'

Ryan took a sip of wine. 'Has Mari showed you the ultrasound pictures yet? Our baby is beautiful.'

Mari's mouth slackened as she turned those big brown eyes of hers to him. They filled and his chest cramped—*please don't cry,* he silently begged—and then they shone. 'Our baby is perfect!' She leapt up to seize the scan photos for her brothers to admire.

Ryan found it hard to believe, but he enjoyed the meal. He didn't doubt that the other two men were reserving their judgement for the time being, but they'd put their overt hostility to one side.

Why?

The answer became increasingly clear as the meal progressed. They adored Marianna and they wanted her to be happy. How could they not love her? She bossed them outrageously, she said deliberately preposterous things to make them laugh, she'd touch their arms in ways that spoke of silent communications he had no knowledge of, but he could see how both men blossomed under her attention, how they relished and treasured it.

In return, she looked up to them so much and loved them so hard that an ache started up deep inside him.

He gripped his cutlery until it bit into him. He wanted her to look up to him like that. He wanted to win her respect. He wanted…

Not love. Never that.

His heart throbbed. Would she love their baby with the same fierceness that she loved her brothers? If she did, then…then this baby didn't need him.

When the children of *another man* took up her heart and her time, though, would her love lose its strength?

A hard rock of resentment lodged in his gut.

If you don't like the idea, pal, marry her yourself.

He shot back in his seat. As if that'd work! Couples shouldn't marry just because they were expecting a baby. It made things ten times worse when they broke up. His parents were proof positive of that. No. He wouldn't be party to making Marianna resent their child more than she inevitably would.

He glanced up to find all eyes at the table on

him. He straightened and cleared his throat. He had no idea what question had just been shot his way, but… 'There's something I've been meaning to raise.'

Marianna stared at him and her eyes suddenly narrowed. Nico gestured for him to continue.

'I understand that harvest time is pretty busy?'

Nico nodded. 'Flat out.'

Ryan glanced first at Marianna and then her brothers. 'Please tell me Marianna won't be working sixty- to eighty-hour weeks.'

'She'll be on maternity leave from August,' Angelo said. 'Nico and I have already discussed it.'

He let out a breath. Good.

'I beg your pardon?' Marianna's eyes flashed and she folded her arms. 'You haven't discussed this with me.'

He stared at her folded arms, at the way her fingers clenched and unclenched, recalled the way she'd flung that vase at him and reached out and took the bowl containing the remainder of the fruit salad they'd had for dessert, pretending to help himself to more before placing it out of her reach. Just to be on the safe side.

'I'll have you know that come harvest I'll still be more than capable of pulling my weight.'

'I need you to monitor the grapes until the end of July,' Nico said. 'But after that I take over.'

'But—'

'No buts.'

Ryan reached a hand towards her, but she ignored it. He soldiered on anyway. 'You're going to be in the last few weeks of your pregnancy. You're going to have a sore back and aching legs.' He wished he could bear those things for her.

'It doesn't make me incapable of doing my job.'

'No one is saying it is,' Angelo said.

She made a wild flourish in the air. 'You cannot exclude me from this!'

Nico seized her hand. 'We're not excluding you, but your health and your *bambino's* health is precious to us. You can sit in a chair in the shade and direct proceedings.'

'You mean I can sit and watch you all work while I put my feet up!'

'You'll still be a part of it.'

She pulled her hand free from Nico's. 'That's bunk and you know it.'

Ryan folded his arms. 'You're going to have to keep an eye on her.'

Nico met Ryan's gaze with a challenge in his

own. 'You could always come back for harvest and keep an eye on her yourself.'

It took an effort not to run a finger around the collar of his shirt. If things went to plan, he'd be neck deep in his assignment for Conti Industries. He might be able to get away for the odd day, but a week, let alone a whole month, would be out of the question. 'I'll see what I can do.' But he already knew he wouldn't be back for the harvest.

'Oh, and now they think I need a babysitter! Fabulous!"

Marianna stalked away to throw herself down on the sofa, where she glowered at them all. Ryan pushed his chair back a tad so he could still include her in the conversation. 'Marianna gave me a tour of the winery the other day.'

'And?' Angelo said.

'You two know what I do, right? That I get called in to turn ailing companies around?'

Nico glared. 'My vineyard is not ailing.'

From the corner of his eye he saw Marianna straighten and turn towards them. 'It's not,' Ryan agreed.

Nico's glare abated but Angelo's interest had been piqued. 'But?'

'You have bottling facilities that stand idle for

much of the year. Did you know that further down the valley there's a brewery that specialises in boutique vinegars? It's an outfit that doesn't have its own bottling facilities. Currently they're sending their stock to Florence for bottling.'

'You're suggesting we could bottle their vinegar?'

Ryan shrugged.

Angelo pursed his lips and glanced at Nico. 'They'd be interested. It'd reduce their transportation costs. And it'd bring additional money into the vineyard with very little effort on our part.'

Nico tapped a finger to the table. 'It'd create more jobs too.'

Angelo and Nico started talking at each other in a rush. Ryan glanced across at Marianna to find her frowning at him, consternation and something else he couldn't identify in the depths of her eyes.

She started when she realised he watched her. Seizing a magazine, she buried her nose in it. But he couldn't help noticing that she didn't turn a single page.

Ryan turned back to the other men. 'I figured it was worth mentioning.' If they were interested in expanding their operations here, it'd be a good place to start.

'How'd you know about this?' Angelo asked.

'It's my job to know.' Old habits died hard. 'I was called in a couple of years ago to overhaul a vineyard in the Barossa Valley. It's one of the things we did to improve their bottom line.'

'And did you save it?'

He shrugged. 'Of course.'

Nico and Angelo started talking ten to the dozen. Marianna came back to the table and joined the debate. Ryan sat back and watched, and hoped he'd proved himself in some small way, hoped he'd eased Marianna's mind and shown her that he and her brothers could get on.

CHAPTER EIGHT

MARIANNA GAVE UP all pretence of conviviality the moment her brothers' broad figures disappeared into the warm darkness of the spring night. Trudging back into the living room, she slumped onto the sofa and stared at the beautiful teddy bear they'd bought for their prospective niece or nephew.

Her eyes filled. Oh, how she loved them!

Ryan clattered about, taking their now-empty coffee cups and wine glasses into the kitchen. 'The evening seemed to go well, don't you think?'

A happy lilt she hadn't heard since Thailand threaded through his voice. She slumped further into the sofa. Of course he'd be happy. *He'd* had a chance to prove his worth and show off his expertise to her brothers.

He started to run hot water into the sink. 'Leave them.' She didn't shout, though it took an effort not to. Who'd have thought he'd have turned out to be such a neat freak? 'I'll do them in the morning.' At least washing dishes was something she *could* do.

Even though she didn't turn around, she sensed his hesitation before he turned the taps off. He moved across to the living area and she could feel him as he drew closer, as if some invisible cord attached her to him. All nonsense!

He picked up the teddy bear, tweaked its ear. 'I think perhaps your brothers are starting to see that I'm not the villain they first thought me.'

No, now they saw him as some kind of super-duper business guru.

He is a business guru.

She ignored that. She could practically see what her brothers now thought. *Poor Ryan—Mari's latest victim who's headed for heartbreak because she's too erratic to settle down.*

She wasn't the one who couldn't settle down. Not that they'd see that. What they'd see was that she'd caught Ryan in her snares—the poor schmuck—and that he was paying a hefty price for it. And... and they'd *admire* him for making the best out of a bad situation.

Having a baby wasn't a bad situation!

'Marianna?'

She started. Had Ryan been talking to her this entire time? She hadn't heard a word of it beyond the fact her brothers didn't hate him any more.

His eyes narrowed on her face. 'You didn't enjoy this evening.'

It was a statement, not a question, so she didn't feel the need to respond.

He eased down into the chair opposite, his frown deepening. 'But I thought you wanted me to get along with your brothers.'

She had. She did! But not at the expense of their opinion of her.

He leaned forward, his expression intent, and something in her chest turned over. She wasn't the one who couldn't settle down. She *ached* to settle down. Not necessarily with Ryan, but... She'd never planned to have a baby on her own. What she'd wanted was to fall in love, get married and then start a family. That sure as heck wasn't going to happen with Ryan. So now she was going to have a baby on her own and it scared her witless.

'This has nothing to do with pregnancy hormones, does it?'

How could he tell? How could he be so attuned to her and yet so far out of her reach?

'No,' she finally said, figuring some kind of response would eventually be expected.

'Do you want to tell me about it?'

She opened her mouth to say no, but the word

refused to emerge. Did she want to talk about it? She blinked when she realised the answer to that question was a rather loud yes.

She moistened her lips and risked another glance into Ryan's face. She'd never spoken to anyone about this before. It seemed too…personal. Besides, all the people she could talk about it with knew Angelo and Nico too.

Ryan knows them now as well.

True, but he'd still be on her side.

Would he? She waved a hand in front of her face. This wasn't about sides. She fixed him with a glare. 'Do you want to know even if it's something you can't fix?'

His eyes didn't leave her face. 'Yes.'

'And if I tell you I don't want you to do anything to try and fix it, because I expect that would only make matters worse, and I don't think I could bear that.'

Slowly he nodded. 'Okay.'

'I meant for tonight to impress Angelo and Nico. I wanted them to recognise my maturity. I wanted to wow them with my graciousness as a hostess. I wanted to prove to them that I'm not an irresponsible idiot or a screw-up!' Her voice had started to rise and she forced it back down. 'But that's certainly not something I managed to accomplish this evening, is it?' She flung out an arm. 'They didn't even trust me to cook the meal properly!'

Ryan's jaw dropped and she leapt up to pace. 'And then you had to go and bring up the whole "Marianna can't work during harvest" thing and all that garbage.' She spun around to glare at him. 'Thank you very much for making me look even worse!'

He shot to his feet and the sheer beauty of his body beat at her. 'The harvest thing? That's because we're all concerned about you.'

She gave up trying to moderate her voice. 'Because none of you think I can look after myself!'

'It's not that at all!'

She folded her arms and kinked a disbelieving eyebrow.

'It's because—' he stabbed a finger at her '—we all want to…' He trailed off, shuffling his feet and looking mildly embarrassed. 'We all want to pamper you,' he mumbled.

It was her jaw that dropped this time. 'I beg your pardon?'

'You're the one who's doing all of the hard work where the baby is concerned. You're the one who has morning sickness, and has had to give up coffee and wine. You're the one who's growing the baby inside you, which probably means you'll get a sore back and sore legs. And then you're the one who's going to have to give birth.'

Ugh. Don't remind her.

'While we—' he slashed a hand through the air '—we're utterly useless! You should know by now that men hate feeling like that. So, while we can't do anything for the baby, we can do things for you—to try and make things easier and nicer for you.'

Ryan felt useless?

'I just…' He grimaced. 'It didn't occur to me that in the process we might be making you feel useless too.'

His explanation put a whole new complexion on the matter. How could she begrudge him—or her brothers—for wanting to help where they could with the baby? She moved a step closer and peered up into his face. 'So…you don't think I'm stupid or that I'm acting irresponsibly?'

'Of course not! I…'

She swung away. 'Of course there's a but.'

'All I was going to say is that I think, in your determination to prove to us all how capable you are, you could be in danger of overdoing it.'

He was talking about that incident with the barrel.

'I did hear you, though—your concern about losing your fitness.'

He had? She turned back.

'I've been trying to find a good time to raise the subject.'

Why? Because she was so touchy she was liable to fly off the handle without warning? She closed her eyes, conceding he might have a point there.

'So I picked up one of these for you.'

She opened her eyes to find him holding out a flyer towards her. She took it. Yoga classes. With an instructor who specialised in yoga for pregnant women. A lump lodged in her throat.

'I just thought you might...' More feet shuffling ensued. 'I mean, if you're not interested, if it's not your thing, then no problem.'

She swallowed the lump. 'No, it's great. I'd have never thought of it, but...it's perfect.'

He didn't smile. He continued to stare at her with a frown in his eyes. 'Mari, your brothers love you. They don't consider you a screw-up.'

Tension shot back through her. 'Those two statements are not mutually exclusive.' She speared the flyer to the fridge with a magnet, before grabbing a glass of water and downing it in one. 'I know my brothers love me.' *That* was why it was so important that she prove herself to them.

Weariness overtook her then. She turned to move back to the sofa, to collapse onto it—to put her feet up and close her eyes—but Ryan blocked her way, anger blazing from the cool depths of his eyes. She backed up a step. 'What?'

'If you believe your brothers think you a screw-up then you're a complete idiot!'

She blinked.

'They adore you!'

'Adoring someone, loving someone,' she found herself yelling back, 'has nothing to do with thinking them capable or adult or believing they're making good decisions about their life!' It didn't mean they thought she'd make a good mother.

'I don't know your brothers very well, but even I can see that's not what they think.'

'Oh, really?' She poked him in the chest. 'What makes you such an expert on the subject? They certainly thought my taking a year off to tour around Australia irresponsible.' Maybe it had been. It'd certainly been indulgent, but she'd needed to spread her wings or go mad. 'And you should've seen the looks on their faces when I told them I was expecting a baby. They definitely thought that an irresponsible mistake of *monumental* proportions.'

She slammed the glass she still held to the bench and pushed past Ryan's intriguing bulk and bristling maleness. His heat and his scent reached around her, making her feel too much, stoking her anger even more. 'So did you!'

'I was wrong! I want this baby. I love this baby!'

She fell onto the sofa, rubbing her temples. Ryan strode across and seized the teddy bear, shook it at her. 'And your brothers love this baby too.'

'You think I don't know that?' She pulled in a breath. 'But I'm not married. This baby wasn't planned.' That last was irresponsible. 'It doesn't mean they don't think I've made a mistake with my life.' And what if they were right? She touched a hand to her stomach. *I'm sorry,* mia topolino.

Ryan sat on the coffee table, knee to knee with her, crowding her. 'So what if they do?'

That was her cue to toss her head and say that it didn't matter, except she didn't have the heart for the lie. She lifted her chin. 'I love them. Their opinions matter to me.'

And what if they were right?

'In this day and age, being a single mother isn't scandalous.'

'I know that, but I live in a conservative part of the world.'

'Your brothers' shock is merely proof of their concern for you, their concern that you'd have no support with the baby—that you would have to do it alone.'

She did have to do it alone. Ryan wanted to be a part of the baby's life, but he didn't want to be part of a family. Ninety per cent of the baby's care would fall to her.

'For heaven's sake, Mari, they don't see you as incapable or a screw-up. Can't you see that? Haven't you worked it out yet? You're the glue that holds this family together.'

He stared at her with such seriousness her heart stopped for a beat. It kicked back in with renewed vigour a moment later. 'What on earth are you talking about?'

'Angelo and Nico obviously have their differences. They want different things from life.'

She snorted. He could say that again.

'Do you think they see each other as inadequate or incompetent?'

She stilled, suddenly seeing where he was going with this.

He leaned over and took her chin in his hand. 'The one thing they can bond over is you. Their love for you, their worry for you and their joy in you—that strengthens their bond and makes you a family.'

He paused. His index finger moved back and forth across her cheek and all Marianna wanted to do was lean into it and purr…to lean into him. An ache started up deep in the centre of her. An ache she knew from experience that Ryan could assuage.

He frowned, his attention elsewhere, and Marianna told herself she was glad he hadn't read her thoughts. 'I don't know what the deal with your parents is, but I've picked up enough to know that you act as a bridge between them and your brothers.'

That was true, but she could only acknowledge it dimly. Ryan continued to frown, but his gaze had caught on her lips and such a roaring hunger stretched through his eyes it made her breath catch and her lips part. His nostrils flared, time stilled. And then he reefed his hand away and shot back.

Not that there was really anywhere he could

move back to—they still sat knee to knee. If she leaned forward, she could run a hand up his leg with seductive intent, a silent invitation that she was almost certain he wouldn't rebuff. Her thigh muscles squeezed in delight at the thought. Deep in the back of her mind, though, a caution sounded. She found herself hovering, caught between a course of action that felt as if it had the potential to change her life.

Sleeping with Ryan will not make him fall in love with you.

Of course it wouldn't. Yet she didn't move away.

'Tell me you've heard all that I've just said.'

She started at his voice.

'About your brothers,' he continued inexorably. 'That you can see they don't think of you as any kind of a failure. They may not agree with every decision you make about your life, just as you may not agree with every decision they make about theirs, but it doesn't mean any of you believe one of the others is a loser or a write-off. It doesn't mean that you don't respect each other.'

Her heart started to pound. 'You truly believe that?'

'I do.' He eased forward again, resting his elbows on his knees. 'Where is this coming from,

Mari? Why haven't you spoken to Angelo or Nico about it?'

She glanced down at her hands. 'They've looked after me since I was a tiny thing. They've spoiled me rotten, indulged me and…I felt as if I'd disappointed them, that I hadn't honoured the faith they'd put in me.' She lifted one shoulder. 'I wanted to prove to them that I was up to the task—that I could do a really good job here at the vineyard *and* be a wonderful mother. But it seemed the harder I tried, the worse I came off. Working so hard suddenly became not looking after myself, or the baby. It seemed to me that everything I did was reinforcing their view of me being incompetent and needing to be looked after.'

'Crazy woman,' he murmured.

'And I didn't feel I should confide all of that in them. They've given me so much—they're the best brothers a girl could ever ask for—and it didn't seem fair to ask more from them, to ask them for assurances.'

'They'd have given them gladly.'

She swallowed. 'A part of me couldn't help feeling they were right.'

His jaw dropped.

She rubbed a hand across her chest. 'How could

I take them to task for their reaction to my baby news when my own initial reaction wasn't much better? Oh, Ryan, joy and excitement weren't my first emotions when I found out I was pregnant. I was frightened…and angry with myself. I wanted it all to go away. I wanted the news to not be true. How dreadful is that?'

He reached out and took her hand 'It's not dreadful. It's human.'

She'd have said exactly the same thing to any one of her girlfriends who found themselves in a similar predicament. She knew that, but…

'Mari, you have to forgive yourself for that. And you have to forgive your brothers for their initial reaction too. And me.' He paused. 'You made a brave decision—an exciting decision—and I can't tell you how grateful I now am for that.'

She could tell he meant every word. And just like that a weight lifted from her.

'You should be proud of yourself.'

Proud?

'You're having a baby. It's exciting. It feels like a miracle.'

Her heart all but stopped. He was right!

She gave up trying to fight temptation then. She leaned forward, took his face in her hands and pressed her lips to his. He froze, but a surge of electricity passed between them, making her tingle all over. She eased back, her heart thumping. 'Thank you.'

He swallowed and nodded. The pulse at the base of his throat pounded and she could feel its rhythm reach right down into the depths of her. Her breath started to come in short sharp spurts. She'd never wanted a man or physical release with such intensity.

Ever.

Maybe it was a pregnancy-hormone thing?

Whatever it was, it was becoming increasingly clear that attempting to explain it, understand it, did nothing to ease its ferocity. She glanced at Ryan, and glanced away again biting her lip. They were both adults. They knew sex didn't mean forever. She tossed her head. If they chose to, they could give each other pleasure in the here and now.

Without giving herself time to think, Marianna slid forward to straddle Ryan's lap.

'What on—?'

Her fingers against his mouth halted his words. 'I want you, Ryan, and I know you want me. I don't really see the point in denying ourselves. Do you?'

She trailed her hand down his chest, relishing

the firm feel of him beneath the cotton of his shirt. He slammed his hand over it, trapping it above the hard thudding of his heart. 'You said if I made love with you here in your real world, that I would break your heart.'

She lifted one shoulder and then let it drop. 'What do I know? Ten minutes ago I was convinced my brothers thought me an incompetent little fool. It appears I was wrong about that.'

For a moment the strength seemed to go out of him. She took advantage of the moment to slide her hands around his shoulders to caress the hair at his nape in a way that she knew drove him wild.

He reached up to remove her hands. 'Mari, I—'

She covered his mouth with her own—open mouth, hot, questing tongue, and a hunger she refused to temper. The taste of him, his heat, drove her wild. With a moan, she sank her teeth into his bottom lip and then laved it with her tongue. Ryan groaned, his hand at the back of her head drawing her closer. His mouth, his lips and his tongue controlled her effortlessly, taming her to his tempo and pace. He drank her in like a starving man and she could only respond with a silent, inarticulate plea that he not stop, that he give her what she needed.

She opened her thighs wider to slide more fully against him and he broke off the kiss to drag in a breath, his chest rising and falling as if he'd run a race.

'We can't do this,' he groaned.

'No?' Marianna peeled off her shirt and threw it to the floor. Her bra followed. She lifted his hands to her breasts, revelling in the way he swallowed, the way he stared at her as if she were the most beautiful woman in the world. 'I understand that you don't want to hurt me, and that's earned you a lot of brownie points, believe me. But at the moment I don't want you honourable. I want you naked and your hands on me, driving me to distraction.'

She moved against his hands. He sucked in a breath. 'Mari…'

She cupped his face, staring into his eyes. 'Just once I want to make love with the father of my child with joy at the knowledge of what we've created.'

He stilled. She swallowed. If he rejected her now she wasn't sure she could bear it. 'It seems to me,' she whispered, 'that would be a good thing to do.'

'Mari…'

She pressed a finger to his lips. 'No promises. I

know that. Just pleasure…and joy. That's all I'm asking.'

She saw the moment he decided to stop fighting it and her heart soared. His eyes gleamed. 'Pleasure, huh?' He ran his hands down her sides, thumbs brushing her breasts and making her bite her lip. 'How much pleasure?'

'I'm greedy,' she whispered.

His hands cupped her buttocks, his fingers digging into her flesh through the thin cotton of her skirt.

She clutched his shoulders, swallowing back a whimper. 'I want a lot of pleasure.'

'A lot, huh?'

His fingers raked down her thighs with deliberate slowness…and with a latent promise of where they would go when he raked them back up again. Marianna started to tremble. Despite the weakness flooding her she managed to toss her head. 'As much as you have to give.'

His eyes darkened with wolfish hunger. 'Whatever the lady wants.' He eased forward to draw her nipple into his mouth and Marianna lost herself in the pleasure.

And the newfound joy that gripped her and seemed to bathe her entire being in sunlight.

* * *

The sound of Ryan's mobile phone ringing woke her. Through half-closed eyes, Marianna watched him reach for it, the long, lean line of his back making her mouth water.

He glanced back towards her and she smiled, sent him a little wave to let him know she was awake and that he didn't need to be extra quiet or leave the room. One side of his mouth kinked up, his eyes darkening as he took in her naked form beneath the sheet. She stretched cheekily, letting the sheet fall to her waist and his grin widened. It made her heart turn over and over. And over.

He finally punched a button on his phone and turned away to concentrate on his call.

A tumbling heart?

Very slowly Marianna sat up, a tight fist squeezing her chest as she continued to stare at Ryan. Her mouth went dry. She drew the sheet back over her. It took all her strength not to pull it right over her head. What on earth had she gone and done?

She didn't want to let this man go. *Ever.*

Her hands fisted. When had it happened? *How* had it happened? Why...?

She swallowed. What did any of that matter? What mattered was that she wanted Ryan to stay here with her forever and be a true partner. She wanted him to share in the day-to-day rearing of their child. She wanted to see him last thing at night and again first thing in the morning.

She *loved* Ryan.

He doesn't want that!

She bit down on her lip to stop from crying out, rubbing a hand across her chest to ease the ache there.

You should never have slept with him.

She waved that away with an impatient movement. Sex had nothing to do with it. Sex wasn't the reason she'd fallen in love with him. His determination to become a good father, his care and consideration of her, the effort he'd put into making a good impression on her brothers, the fact he wanted her to be happy—they were the reasons she'd fallen in love with him. She passed a hand across her eyes. It seemed for the last week she'd been doing her best to hide from that fact.

What good was hiding, though?

And yet, what good was facing the truth? He loved his work more than he'd ever love her.

'I'll be there as soon as I can!'

She snapped to at Ryan's words. 'What's wrong?' she demanded, pushing her own concerns aside at his grim expression and the greyness that hovered in the lines around his mouth.

'My mother has been taken ill. I need to return to Sydney as soon as I can.'

He had a mother?

She hadn't realised she'd said that out loud until he said, 'And a father. They divorced when I was young. They both have new families now.'

Which meant he had siblings. And yet…amidst this big family Ryan managed to be a lone wolf?

She surged out of bed, pulling on her dressing gown to race into the spare bedroom after him where he'd set about throwing clothes into his suitcase. She wanted to hold him, chase that haggard look from his face. 'What can I do?'

He stilled from hauling on a clean pair of suit trousers. He zipped them up and then moved to touch her face with one hand. 'I just want you to look after yourself and the baby.'

If he left now she'd have lost him forever. She'd never get the opportunity to win his love.

It could be for the best—a quick, clean break. But…

Lone wolf.

If something terrible happened—if he received dreadful news or, heaven forbid, if his mother died—who would be there to comfort him, to offer him support and anything else he needed?

She moistened her lips, pulling the dressing gown about her all the more tightly. 'Can I come with you?'

Ryan froze at Marianna's request. He turned. 'Why would you want to do that?'

She pushed a strand of gloriously mussed hair behind her ears. 'I didn't know you had a family.'

He didn't. *They* were a family and *he* was an outsider. They were simply people he happened to be related to by blood.

So why is your heart pounding nineteen to the dozen at the thought of your mother lying in a hospital bed?

He pushed that thought away and focused on Marianna again. She swallowed. 'I'd like to meet them. They'll be a part of our baby's life and—'

'A small part,' he said. 'A *very* small part.'

She thrust out her chin and he found himself having to fight the urge to kiss her. 'You've met my family.'

'Not your parents.'

'But you will,' she promised. 'Just as soon as I can arrange it.'

How could she so easily make him feel part of something—like her family—when there was no place for him in it? It had to be an illusion.

'I don't mean to be gone long, Marianna. I need to be back in Rome in two weeks at the latest—' preferably sooner '—to settle the contract I've been working on.'

One of her shoulders lifted and then she surged forward to grip his hand. 'Ryan, we're friends, right?'

Were they? It was what he'd been striving for, but the word didn't seem right somehow.

Because you slept with her, you idiot.

He shook that off. He couldn't regret last night if he tried his hardest. He'd only regret it if it'd hurt Marianna.

He stared down into her eyes—their warmth and generosity caught at him. Her gaze held his, steadily. Neither pain nor regret reached out to squeeze his heart dry, only concern. Concern for him. He swallowed. Friendship might not be the right word, but it didn't mean he couldn't continue to strive for exactly that.

'Ryan, I'd like to be there for you if you receive bad news.'

It took an effort to lock his knees against the

weakness that shook through him when he realised the kind of bad news she referred to. It didn't make sense. He was barely a part of his mother's life. Or his father's. Family made no sense to him at all.

But it made sense to Marianna. That might come in handy. She might be able to help him to navigate the tricky waters ahead.

She attempted a smile. 'I might even be able to make myself useful.'

He wanted her to come with him. The thought shocked him.

It didn't mean anything. It *couldn't* mean anything.

He pulled in a breath. He supposed he'd have to tell them all at some point that he was going to become a father. That would be easier with Marianna by his side.

Finally he nodded. 'Okay, but I want to be on the first available flight out of Rome for Sydney.'

She raced back towards her bedroom. 'I'll be ready!'

CHAPTER NINE

'TELL ME ABOUT your family.'

Ryan fought a grimace as he shifted on his seat—a generous business class seat that would recline full length when he wanted to sleep. Sleep was the furthest thing from his mind at the moment, though. He wished planes had on-board gyms. 'What do you want to know?'

'Do both of your parents live in Sydney?'

In stark contrast to him, Marianna looked cool and comfortable and *very* delectable. He tried to tamp down on the ache that rose up through him. 'Yes.'

She stared as if waiting for more. He lifted a hand. 'What?'

'Sydney is a big city, Ryan.'

Right. 'They live in the eastern suburbs. In adjoining suburbs, would you believe? It's where they grew up.'

She pursed her lips and he waited for her next

question with a kind of fatalistic resignation. He supposed it'd help pass the time.

'You said they divorced when you were young. How old were you?'

'Four.'

'And…and did they share custody?'

Her questions started to make sense. He shook his head. 'I went to live with my maternal grandmother.'

She smiled and he couldn't explain why, but it bathed him in warmth. It made him very glad to have her sitting beside him. 'The grandmother who taught you to make curtains?'

'The very one.'

'Where were your parents? What were they doing?'

'They went their separate ways to "find" themselves.' He couldn't stop himself from making mocking inverted commas in the air.

She turned more fully in her seat to face him, crossing her legs in the process, and her skirt rode up higher on her thigh. He stared at the perfectly respectable amount of flesh on display, remembering how he'd run his hands up her thighs last night…and how he'd followed with his mouth. He wished he could do that right now—lose himself in the pleasure of being in her arms, give himself over to the generous delights of her body.

'That makes them sound very young. How old were they?'

He pulled himself back. He had to stop thinking about making love with Marianna. It couldn't happen again. Already it was starting to feel too concentrated, too...intimate. Like an affair. He didn't do affairs. He did one-night stands. He did ships passing in the night. He did short-term dalliances. Somehow, from the wreck of his and Marianna's entanglement, he had to fashion a friendship that would endure the coming years.

Boring.

He stiffened. It was the responsible route. The *essential* route. And like everything else he'd turned his hand to, if he worked at it hard enough he would achieve it.

'Ryan?'

He shook himself, dragged a hand down his face. 'They were eighteen when they had me.'

'Eighteen?' Her eyes widened. 'I'm twenty-four and most days I don't feel ready for parenthood. But eighteen? Just...wow.'

He'd started to realise that parenthood frightened her as much as it frightened him. It was why he

had to remain close and keep things pleasant between them. When motherhood and the responsibility of raising a child overwhelmed Marianna,
when it lost its gloss, he'd be there to take over.

'How long did you live with your grandmother?'

'Until I was nineteen.'

Her jaw dropped. She shuffled a little closer,
drenching him with her sweet scent. 'You never
lived with your parents again?'

He stared at the back of the seat in front of him.
'I visited with them.' But he'd never fitted in. It had
always been a relief to return home to his grandmother. He'd only kept up the visits because his
grandmother had insisted. For her he'd have done
anything.

'So, you and your parents, you're not what one
would call…close?'

'Not close at all.'

'But…'

He turned and met her gaze.

'You've dropped everything to go to your
mother.'

'That's not a mystery.' He turned back to the
front. 'I'm the one with the money, and money
talks. I can make things happen.'

'Like?'

'Get in the best doctors, fly in the top specialists, fast-track test results—that kind of thing.' He'd do that—make sure everything was in place for his mother—and then he'd hightail it back to Italy to wrap up the Conti contract.

Marianna blinked and then frowned. 'That's terrible!'

It took an effort of will to stop his lips from twisting. 'It's the way the world works.'

She was silent for a moment. 'I meant it's terrible that's the way you feel, that that's the role you see for yourself in your family.'

Maybe he should've taken the time to pretty it all up for her, except she'd see it all for herself soon enough.

'You have siblings?'

Tiredness washed through him. 'Yes.' He didn't give her the time to ask how many. 'My father is onto marriage number three. He has a daughter to wife number two and two boys with wife number three. My mother has one of each with her second husband. The eldest of them is twenty-two—my mother's daughter who has a toddler of her own. The youngest is my father's son who is thirteen.'

'Wow. Where do you spend Christmas?'

'*Not* in Australia.'

She nodded, but the sadness in her eyes pierced him, making his chest throb. 'Why don't you get some sleep?' he suggested. She must be bone-tired. 'You didn't get a whole lot of rest last night.'

The sudden wicked grin she flashed him kicked up his pulse, making his blood pump faster. 'I wish I was getting next to no sleep tonight for exactly the same reason.'

So did he. Except... *No affairs.* He knew she'd said no promises, but... 'Do we need to talk about last night?' Did they need to double-check that they were still on the same page?

She smiled a smile so slow and seductive he had to bite back a groan. 'We can if you like,' she all but purred. 'There was a manoeuvre of yours that I particularly relished. It was when you—'

He pressed a finger to her lips, his heart pounding so hard the sound of it filled his ears. 'Stop it!' But a laugh shot out of him at the same time. 'You're incorrigible. Give me some peace, woman, and go to sleep.'

'On one condition.'

'Anything!'

'Kiss me first.'

Her eyes darkened with an unmistakable challenge. He leaned towards her. 'Do you think I won't?'

She leaned in closer still. 'I'm very much hoping you will.'

He seized her lips in a fierce kiss, not questioning the hunger that roared through him. He didn't gather her close. He didn't even cup her face. She didn't reach out a hand to touch him either, but a kiss he'd thought would be all fire and sass changed when her lips parted and softened and moved beneath his with a warmth and a relish that shifted something inside him. He went to move away, but her lips followed and he found himself unable to stop; he surged forward again to plunder and explore that softness and warmth, to pull it into himself. The kiss went on and on... and on, as if she had an endless supply of something he desperately needed.

Eventually they drew apart. 'Mmm...yum.' Her tongue ran across her bottom lip as if savouring the taste of him there.

He had no words. All he could do was stare at her. She reclined her seat. She reached out a hand to his knee; her touch... He couldn't find the right word for it—comforting, reassuring? 'Put your seat back and keep me company.'

He covered her with a blanket first and then did as she bid.

'Close your eyes,' she murmured, not even opening hers to see if he obeyed.

After a moment, he did. He could feel sleep coming to claim him and suddenly realised that Marianna's kiss had stolen some of the sting from his soul. He had no idea what it meant. He breathed air into lungs that didn't feel quite so cramped and drifted off to sleep, promising himself he'd work it out later.

He slept for three hours. Not just dozed, but slept. He woke and stretched, feeling strangely refreshed. He checked his phone, but there weren't any messages.

Half an hour later, Marianna stirred. 'Sleep well?' he asked when she opened her eyes.

'Perfectly,' she declared, sitting up. 'You?'

He nodded.

She sent him a grin that made his blood sizzle. 'Wanna kiss me again in a little while when I'm ready for another snooze?'

He laughed, but shook his head—trying to ignore the ache that surged through him. 'We can't keep doing that.'

She reached for the bottle of water the stewardess had left for her. 'I expect you're right, but I mean to enjoy it while it lasts.'

How long would it last? More to the point, how long did he want it to last? Could they maybe make love one more time without Marianna's heart becoming entangled? Twice more? He'd give up a lot to have another week like they had in Thailand.

But not at the expense of screwing up friendship and fatherhood.

His seat suddenly felt as hard and unyielding as a boulder. He excused himself and bolted to the rest room to dash cold water onto his face, to stare at himself in the mirror and order himself to keep his hands and lips to himself.

When he couldn't remain in there any longer without exciting comment, he forced himself back to his seat. 'Why don't you tell me about your parents?' he suggested, hoping conversation would keep his raging hormones in check. 'It seems that you and your brothers have different opinions on the subject.'

She nodded. 'Mamma and Papà have a very… tempestuous relationship. They're both very passionate people.'

Sounded like a recipe for disaster to him.

'When we were growing up there were a lot of… um…rather loud discussions.'

'Fights.'

She wrinkled her nose. 'A bit of shouting…a bit of door-slamming.'

He recalled the way she'd thrown that vase at him.

Uh-huh, utter nightmare. He thanked the stewardess when she brought him the drink he'd requested.

'They divorced once. And then they remarried.'

He choked on his drink. 'But…why?'

She lifted one slim shoulder. 'It's the same now. They're currently in America, but their relationship is as fiery as it ever was. They're forever threatening to leave each other, storming out for a few days before coming back. On again off again.' She gave a low laugh. 'They can't live without each other. It's wildly romantic.'

He stared at her. 'Romantic? Are you serious? It sounds like a nightmare.'

She leaned back, her gaze narrowing. 'Maybe it's a male thing. You seem to have jumped to the same conclusion as Angelo and Nico.'

They were obviously men of sense. 'You say

they can't live without each other. Seems to me they can't live *with* each other.'

She shook her head. He tried not to let her dancing curls distract him. 'The intensity of their love drives them to distraction. So, yes, I think that romantic. Boredom is death to a relationship and while you can say a lot of things about my parents the one thing you can't accuse them of is being bored…or boring.'

Was that the kind of relationship she wanted? Did she mean to marry a man and raise Ryan's child in a battleground? 'Boredom?' he spat. 'I'd take it over never being able to relax or wind down. What on earth is wrong with contentment?'

Her face wrinkled up as if she'd just sucked on a lemon. 'Oh, yay, that sounds like fun.'

'The way your parents act, it's immature. Sounds as if neither one of them has the ability to compromise and I don't see what's particularly loving or romantic about that.'

She glared at him. 'I'm starting to think you wouldn't know love if it jumped up and bit you on the nose. You avoid love and connection as if it's some kind of plague, so you'll have to excuse me if I don't take you as an expert on the topic.'

She had a point, but… 'You'd really prefer to

have the kind of screaming match that leaves you shaken and in tears than...than smiles and easiness and happiness?'

'It's not an either-or situation.' She folded her arms. 'Besides, I hear that make-up sex is the best.'

'Is it all about sex with you?'

'Oh, excuse me while I roll my eyes out loud! I like sex.' She thrust out her chin. 'And I have no intention of apologising for that.'

'You'd have that kind of crazy, outrageous relationship even if it made the people around you miserable?'

'My parents' relationship didn't make *me* miserable.'

'I expect that's because Angelo and Nico shielded you from the worst of it. It certainly made them miserable. What if it makes our child miserable?'

Her eyes flashed. 'Oh, no, you don't! You are not going to control me or my future romantic liaisons by means of some kind of twisted maternal guilt you feel you have the right to impose on me. I will marry whomever I choose, Ryan, and it will have nothing to do with you.' With that she grabbed a magazine and promptly set about ignoring him.

He had absolutely no right to tell her who she should or shouldn't marry but...

Why couldn't she just remain single?

With a groan, he dragged both hands back through his hair. Why on earth hadn't he simply forgone the small talk and kissed her again?

Marianna stood the moment Ryan returned to the waiting room, twisting her hands together and searching his face. All they'd known prior to arriving at the hospital was that Stacey, Ryan's mother, had snapped a tendon in her calf playing squash and that a blood clot had formed at the site of the injury. The doctors were doing everything they could to dissolve the clot, but so far it hadn't responded. If the clot—or any part of it—moved and made its way to her heart or brain...

Marianna suppressed a shudder, and made a vow to never play squash again. 'How is she?'

Ryan didn't answer. His pallor squeezed her heart. She reached out and wrapped her arm through his. 'The doctors are doing everything they can.'

He nodded and swallowed and her heart bled for him. He might not be close to his family, but he loved his mother. That much was evident.

'She'd like to see you.'

She eased away to stare up into his face. 'Me?'

'The doctor said that's fine, but she's only allowed one visitor at a time and she's not to get excited or upset.'

No excitement and no upsetting the woman. Right. She pressed a hand to her stomach. 'Did you tell her about the baby?'

He nodded. 'That's why she wants to meet you.'

She moistened her lips. 'In my experience, news about a baby definitely falls under the heading of exciting.' And depending on the situation and the person being told, fraught with the possibility of distress and worry.

'She's fine with it.' He pushed her towards the door of his mother's room. 'Go and introduce yourself and then we can get the hell out of here.'

She didn't remonstrate with him. For pity's sake, she'd done enough of that on the plane! Not a smart move when trying to make oneself an attractive long-term romantic prospect. But behind his impatience and assumed insensitivity she recognised his fear. She wished she could do something to allay it.

He frowned. 'You don't want to meet her?'

She shook herself. 'I do, yes, very much.' She straightened her shirt and smoothed down her skirt, wishing she'd had an opportunity to at least shower before meeting Ryan's mother. Ryan collapsed onto a chair and rested back, his eyes closed. He must be exhausted. As soon as she'd visited a little with Stacey she'd get him to a hotel somewhere where he could rest up.

Pulling in a breath, she padded down the hallway and tapped on Stacey's door before entering. 'Mrs White, um, sorry… Mrs Pickering?'

'You must be Marianna. Do come in and, please, call me Stacey.'

Ryan had Stacey's colouring, and her eyes. For some reason it put Marianna at ease. 'It's lovely to meet you.' She took the hand Stacey held out to her, pressed it warmly, before taking a seat at the side of the bed. 'I've been ordered to not wear you out.'

Stacey sighed. 'It seems a whole lot of fuss and bother for nothing.'

That sounded like Ryan too. Marianna glanced down her nose and lifted an eyebrow.

Stacey laughed. 'I know, I know. It's not nothing, but the fact of the matter is I'm not even in that much pain and all of this sitting around is driving me mad.'

She sounded *a lot* like Ryan.

'You're having a baby.'

Straight to the heart of the matter. 'Yes.'

'That's lovely news.' The other woman nodded. 'A baby… That's exactly what Ryan needs.'

Marianna didn't know what to say.

'You care about my son?'

She didn't bother dissembling. Stacey was Ryan's mother and her baby's grandmother. 'Yes, I do.'

Their eyes met and held. They both knew that her *caring* about Ryan could end in heartbreak.

'I made a grave mistake when I separated from my then husband and left Ryan with his grandmother. She loved Ryan to bits, but I only ever meant to leave him with her for a couple of weeks.'

Marianna opened her mouth to ask why she hadn't gone back for him—how had two weeks turned into fifteen years—but she closed it again.

'My heart was broken,' Stacey continued, 'and it took me a long time to recover.'

Marianna could understand that, but she still wouldn't have given up her child.

Stacey met Marianna's gaze. 'I was crippled with self-doubt and a lack of confidence. I felt I'd made a mess of everything. I'd hurt Ryan's father. I'd disappointed my mother. I thought I must be a bad person and I convinced myself that I'd ruin Ryan's life. That is the single biggest regret I have.'

Marianna understood self-doubt all too well, and Stacey would've been even younger than Marianna was now. She reached out and touched Stacey's arm. 'You were young. It was all such a long time ago. It's in the past—'

'No, it's not.' Her gaze didn't drop. 'It's there between us every time I see him. He's not trusted me since. He's never forgiven me.'

Her heart burned for the both of them. But… What did Stacey want her to do—to reconcile Ryan with his past? She could try, but—

'I'm telling you this to help you understand my son a little better, Marianna. Since his grandmother died I'm not sure he's trusted anyone, but I think he might trust you. At least a little.'

She hoped he did.

'Maybe you'll be able to find it in your heart to make allowances for him when he doesn't act as emotionally invested as you'd like.'

Therein lay the rub. She wanted—needed— Ryan's wholehearted involvement, his complete commitment. She wasn't a masochist. She couldn't settle for anything less.

Ryan liked everyone to see him as cool and controlled, but she knew the passion that lurked beneath the impassive veneer. She lifted her chin. She and Ryan, they didn't have to end in heartbreak. She could win his love yet. The first step, though, would be to reconcile him with his family. It wouldn't be easy, of course. But it couldn't be impossible, could it?

'I still don't see why we have to stay at Rebecca's,' Ryan muttered.

'Because she asked us,' Marianna returned.

He opened his mouth.

'And because she's going to be our child's aunt. It's natural she should want to get to know me, and I'd like to get to know her.'

Yesterday, Marianna had walked out of Stacey's hospital room to find a large portion of Ryan's family in the waiting room—his stepfather, as well as his sister, her husband and their little girl. When Rebecca, Ryan's sister, had invited them to stay with her, Marianna had jumped at the invitation.

'What if I don't want these people to be part of my child's life?'

'Lulu, honey, don't put that in your mouth.' Marianna jumped up from her seat on the park bench to take the stick from the toddler's hand and to wipe her mouth, before distracting her with a bright red toy truck, helping her to push it through the sand.

She'd dragged Ryan out to the little park across the road from Rebecca's house on the pretext of taking his niece, Lulu, for a little outing.

In reality, though, she'd just wanted to get Ryan out of the house before he exploded—to give them all a bit of a breather. She took her seat on the bench again. 'I like your sister.'

'So that settles it, does it? I hate to point this out to you, but you might find it difficult to become best buds with my sister when she lives here and you live in Monte Calanetti.'

She swung to him, loathing the tone he'd assumed. 'And I hate to point out that it's not Rebecca's fault that your parents separated and left you with your grandmother.'

His eyes turned to chips of ice. 'Very mature.'

'My point exactly! Rebecca is making every effort to forge a relationship with you and you're freezing her out. Why?'

He dragged a hand down his face and she suddenly wished she'd spat those home truths out with a little more kindness. 'I have never felt a part of these people's lives.'

'I know,' she whispered. 'Life gets messy and

people don't always know the right way to deal with things. But you're an adult now, Ryan. You can choose to become a part of this family.'

He stared at her. His lips twisted in mockery, but she recognised pain in the hidden depths of his eyes. 'What's the point?'

She couldn't speak for a moment. She turned away to check on Lulu. 'Belonging is its own reward,' she finally managed.

He shook his head. 'Lone wolf.'

'Family is a gift you can give our baby.' Couldn't he see that? 'The more people who love it, the better.'

'You mean the more people there will then be in the world with the potential to hurt it, let it down... betray it.'

She shot to her feet. He could *not* be serious. She started to shake. 'I will not let you turn our child into an emotional cripple...into an emotional coward.'

He turned those cold eyes to her. 'And I won't let you turn it into an emotion junkie.'

That was what he thought of her? She turned away to check again on Lulu, who was perfectly content crawling in the sand with her toy truck. Marianna pulled in a breath and closed her eyes.

This wasn't about her. It was about Ryan. She could tell how much he hated being here—in Australia, at Rebecca's—but...

He'd organised a top specialist for his mother at his own expense. Rebecca had told her that her husband owed his job in a top-flying computer graphics company to Ryan's machinations. Rebecca owed her university education to him. They admired him, respected him, and looked up to him. He looked out for them—made sure they had everything they needed—yet he continued to hold himself aloof from them.

He might not want to acknowledge it, but he loved this family that he kept at arm's length.

She sat again. 'Rebecca loves you.'

He stiffened.

'And treating her the way you do...' She used his earlier words against him. 'It hurts her, lets her down, betrays her.'

He stood, his eyes wild. 'That's not true!'

'Yes, it is. Now sit back down and don't frighten the baby.'

He sat. His hands clenched. 'I don't mean to hurt anyone.'

The coldness had melted from him. It took all her strength not to take him in her arms. 'Rebecca would never hurt our child,' she said instead. 'She'd love it, protect it, support it.'

Lulu came over and pulled herself upright using Ryan's trouser leg. She grinned up at him, slapping her hand to his knee in time to her garbled, 'Ga, ga, ga!'

'I, uh…' He glanced at Marianna, who kept her mouth firmly shut. He glanced back at the toddler, lifted a shoulder. 'Ga, ga, ga?' he said back.

Lulu chortled as if he were the funniest man alive. Just for a moment he grinned and it reached right down inside her. This man deserved to be surrounded by a big, loving family.

Lulu wobbled and then fell down onto her diaper-clad bottom. Her face crumpled and she started to cry.

His hands fluttered. 'Uh, what do I do?'

Was he talking about Lulu or Rebecca? Either way, the advice would be almost the same. 'You pick her up and cuddle her. Cuddles make most things better.'

Gingerly he picked Lulu up, sat her on his knee and patted her back, jiggling his knee up and down. She gave him a watery smile and Marianna's chest cramped as she watched him melt. She crossed her fingers and silently ordered Lulu to keep working her magic.

CHAPTER TEN

MARIANNA GLANCED UP from slicing salad vegetables when Ryan strode into the kitchen.

'Hey, Ryan,' Rebecca said from her spot by the grill where she turned marinated chicken breasts.

Ryan stole a cherry tomato from the salad bowl. 'Is there anything I can do?'

Marianna would've smacked his hand except she sensed the effort it took him to appear casual and relaxed.

'Not much to do,' his sister said. 'I think we have it all under control.'

He reached into the salad bowl again, and this time she slapped the back of his hand with the flat of her knife. 'Ow!'

'You can stop eating all the salad, for one thing.'

His gaze speared to hers. He visibly relaxed at her smile. He turned back to Rebecca. 'I kind of figured there'd be nothing useful I could do in here so I went out and bought this.'

He handed her a bottle of wine. Her eyes widened when she saw the label. 'Ooh, you really shouldn't have, but...nice!'

He shoved his hands in his pockets. 'I thought you deserved a treat after everything you've done—dealing with Mum, putting us up.'

Rebecca's chin came up. 'We're family, Ryan.'

He took the bottle of wine from her and poured out two glasses. He handed her one. He raised his own. 'Yes, we are.' Her eyes widened, a smile trembled on her lips, and then she touched her glass to his.

After his first sip, he set his glass down and poured Marianna a big glass of mineral water, complete with lemon slice and ice. With his hands on her shoulders, he shepherded her around the kitchen bench and into a chair at the kitchen table, before taking over the slicing of a cucumber.

Marianna didn't make a single peep about not feeling useful. Instead, she held her breath as she watched Ryan begin to forge a relationship with his sister.

He glanced around. 'Where's my...ahem... where's Lulu?'

Rebecca laughed. 'Your niece is having a much-needed nap. And you are *not* disturbing her.'

'Wouldn't dream of it.'

'She has you wrapped around her little finger.'

'Can't deny that I've taken to the little tyke.' He paused, pursed his lips. 'You know, Lulu's going to be less than three years older than her yet-to-be-born cousin. They could—you know—' he lifted a shoulder '—become great mates.'

Rebecca stilled and Marianna saw her blink hard. She wanted to jump up and down, cheer, dance around the kitchen.

Rebecca simply nodded. 'Wouldn't that be great?'

Ryan focused doubly hard on slicing a red capsicum, and nodded.

A moment later his mobile rang. He fished it out, listened intently, murmured a few words and then shoved it back into his pocket. 'That was the hospital. The clot has started to dissolve and if all goes as the specialist hopes, Mum will be released in a couple of days.'

Rebecca clapped a hand to her chest and closed her eyes. 'Thank heaven.'

Ryan let out a long, slow breath and then lifted his glass. 'To the prognosis being correct.'

They drank. When he set his glass down, Ryan rolled his shoulders. 'Do you think you could keep an eye out for a suitable property for me?'

Marianna stilled with her glass of mineral water halted halfway to her mouth. Had she just heard him right?

'Sure.' Rebecca—a real estate agent—nodded. 'What kind of property did you have in mind?'

Marianna's heart started to thud. Did Ryan mean to give up his anonymous hotel rooms for a real home?

'Here in Sydney?' Rebecca asked.

Ryan nodded.

'Preferred suburbs?'

Marianna waited for him to request some swish apartment overlooking Sydney harbour.

He threw the freshly cut capsicum into the salad bowl. 'The eastern suburbs are fine by me.'

'Apartment? Villa? Town house?' Rebecca shot each option at him.

'I want a house,' he said. 'With a yard.'

Marianna choked and had to thump her chest to get herself back under control.

He glanced at her. 'A child needs a yard, right? A place to run around and play?'

She nodded.

He frowned. 'You won't mind me bringing the baby to visit?'

She suspected she kind of would, but... 'Of

course not.' She wanted their baby to know his family. 'You might have to wait until he or she is weaned first, though.'

'You could come too.'

If she had her way, that was exactly what would happen—the three of them coming here as a family. She dabbed her napkin to her mouth. When Ryan decided to do something—like become an involved father or build bridges with his sister—he certainly did it with gusto. If possible, it only made her love him more.

'Are you planning on going to the hospital today?' Marianna asked Ryan the next morning.

He didn't glance up from his newspaper. 'I don't think so.'

She bit her tongue to stop from asking, *Why not?*

They'd slept late—probably due to jet lag—and currently had the house to themselves. Rebecca's note had said she'd gone up to the hospital. Marianna took a sip of her decaffeinated coffee. Setting her mug back to the table, she ran her finger around its rim. 'Your grandmother lived close to here?'

'On the other side of the main street.' One shoulder lifted. 'Probably a ten- or fifteen-minute walk from here.'

'A walk would be nice. So would a big fat piece of cake.'

He glanced up. 'You want to see where my grandmother lived?'

'I want to see where *you* lived.'

'Why?'

She wanted each and every insight into him that she could get. She wanted to understand why he'd exiled himself from his family. She wanted every weapon she could lay her hands on to make sure he didn't exile himself from her.

Or their baby.

No. Their baby already had his heart.

But she didn't. Not yet.

And she couldn't simply blurt out, *I've fallen deeply and completely in love with you and I want to understand you so that I can work out how to make you fall in love with me.*

She imagined the look on his face if she did, and it almost made her laugh.

And then she imagined the fallout from such an admission and she wanted to throw up.

Ryan's frown deepened. 'You looked for a moment as if you might laugh and now you look as if you want to cry.'

Oops. 'Pregnancy hormones.'

'Breathing exercises,' he ordered.

She feigned doing breathing exercises until she had herself back under control. 'I'd like to see where you grew up. You've seen my world and now I'd like to see yours.' A sudden thought occurred to her. 'But if you'd rather not revisit your past then that's okay too.' She didn't mean to raise demons for him. 'I just…' She wrinkled her nose. 'It's probably a bit selfish of me, but knowing all this stuff—your life here in Australia—it'll make it easier for me when our child does come out here for visits.'

His face softened. 'You're frightened by how much you'll miss it?'

She nodded.

'Me too. I mean, how much I'll miss it when I'm away with work.'

Did that mean…? 'Are you planning on buying a home in Monte Calanetti too?'

He nodded and it occurred to her that she could use this baby as leverage, to convince him that marriage would be the best thing, but… She didn't want him to marry her for any other reason than that he couldn't live without her.

'You could come on the visits to Australia too if you wanted, Mari. You'd be very welcome. My family adores you.'

It was his adoration she craved, not his family's—as much as she liked them. 'You forget that I have a job.'

'I'll pay you so much child support you'll never have to work again.'

'You forget that I like my job.'

He stared at her for a long moment. With a curse he seized their mugs and took them to the sink. 'Don't worry. I haven't forgotten that you don't want me cramping your style.'

A thrill shot through her at his scowl. If the thought of her with another man made him look like that, then… She left the thought unfinished, but in her lap she crossed her fingers. 'So, are you going to show me your grandmother's house or not?'

'I expect if I want any peace I'll have to,' he grumbled.

'And buy me a piece of cake on the way home?'

He battled a smile. 'And what do I get in return?'

She didn't bother hiding her grin. 'Peace.'

'Deal!'

This time he laughed and it lifted her heart. She could make him laugh. She could drive him wild in bed. She'd helped him make peace with his sister. *And* she was going to have his baby. Surely it was just a matter of time before he fell in love with her?

She crossed her fingers harder.

Ryan pulled to a halt and gestured to the simple brick bungalow. 'There it is.' The house he'd grown up in. He watched a myriad expressions cross Marianna's face. It was easier looking at her than looking at the house and experiencing the gut-wrenching loss of his grandmother all over again.

Avid curiosity transformed into a genuine smile. 'It's tiny!'

He glanced up and down the street. 'Once upon a time this entire suburb was composed of these two-bedroom miners' cottages.' Most had long since been knocked down, replaced with large, sprawling, modern homes.

'It's charming! It looks like a proper home…just like my cottage.'

He glanced back and waited for pain to hit him. It did, but it didn't crush him. He let out a careful breath.

Marianna swung to him. 'Don't you agree?'

She was right. Gran's house did remind him of her cottage.

'Was the garden this tidy when you were growing up?'

'Keeping this garden tidy was how I earned my pocket money.' That and stacking shelves at the local supermarket.

A teasing smile lit her lips and it tugged at his heart. 'So...were you a tearaway? A handful? Did you turn your grandmother's hair prematurely grey?'

He pressed his lips together as the old regrets rose up to bite him. 'Definitely a handful.' She didn't look at him, too interested in the house and garden, and he was glad for it. 'I was...rebellious.'

A laugh tinkled out of her. 'Surely not.'

He wanted to close his eyes, but he set his shoulders instead. Marianna ought to know the truth. 'As a teenager I fell in with a bad crowd. I was expelled from school.'

She spun around. Her mouth opened and closed, but no sound came out. He didn't blame her. 'My grandmother was a saint.'

'Expelled?'

He nodded.

'From school?'

'That's right.'

'But look at you now!' She suddenly seemed to realise that her shock might be making him uncomfortable. She tutored her face to something he figured she hoped was more polite. 'You, uh… certainly turned your life around.'

Not soon enough for his grandmother to have seen it.

She glanced back at the house and swallowed. 'I wish I could've met her.'

He hesitated for a moment before pulling his wallet from his pocket and removing a photo. Silently he handed it across to her.

She stared at it for a long moment, ran a finger across the face. 'You have her smile.'

He did?

She smiled at the photo before handing it back. 'I hope our baby has that smile.'

He hoped their child had Marianna's love of life, her exuberance, and her generosity.

He blinked, his head rearing back. Where had that come from? He put the photo away. Those things were all well and good as long as the child also had his logical thinking and the ability to read a situation quickly and accurately.

'Your grandmother helped you find your way again?'

Heaviness settled across his chest. 'In a manner of speaking. When she died, I realised I hadn't honoured her enough in life.'

She pressed a hand to her chest, her eyes filling. 'Oh!'

After a couple of moments she slid her arm through his and rested her head against his shoulder. It wasn't a sexy move but a companionable one and it immediately made him feel a little less alone.

'So you decided to honour her memory?'

He nodded.

'That was a good thing to do,' she whispered. 'I think she'd be proud of you.'

He hoped so. 'She always claimed I had a quick mind that I shouldn't waste.'

She eased away from him. 'I meant I think she'd be pleased with the way you're accepting your responsibilities as a prospective father.'

He swallowed.

'And with the way you're building a relationship with Rebecca.'

That would definitely have eased her heart. 'I...' He shrugged and then glanced at her helplessly.

'That thing you said yesterday about my distance hurting Rebecca, I…'

He dragged a hand back through his hair, that heaviness settling all the more firmly over him. He stared at the front door of his grandmother's old house and wished with everything he had that he could walk in there and talk with her one last time.

'You didn't know you were hurting her. It wasn't something you were doing on purpose.'

'But now that I do know I can't just…' He turned to face her fully. 'I can't ignore it. I can't keep hurting her.'

She reached up to touch his cheek. 'You're a good man, you know that?'

She made him feel like a good man. Rebecca's smile yesterday when they'd clinked wine glasses had made him feel like a good man too. Mari's hand against his cheek, her softness, made his heart start to pound, alerted all of his senses until they were dredged with the scent of her. It took all of his strength not to turn his mouth and press a kiss into the palm of her hand.

Kissing her would not be a good thing to do.

It'd be glorious.

He tried to shut that thought off.

She kept her hand there a beat and a half longer

than she should've and it near killed him to resist her silent invitation. When she moved back a step, though, he had to grind back a groan of frustration.

'Thank you.'

He moistened suddenly dry lips. 'For what?'

'For showing me this.' She gestured to the house. 'For giving me a little insight into your background.'

She stared at him as if he were… As if he were a hero! His stomach lurched. He was no hero. And the last thing he needed was Marianna getting starry-eyed. *You should never have slept with her.* For the rest of their lives they'd be inextricably linked through their child. It only seemed right they should know each other, but… An ache stretched behind his eyes. He had to bring a halt to this right now. 'Friends, right?'

Her smile slipped a little and it was like a knife sliding in between his ribs.

He soldiered on. 'This sharing of confidences, it's what friends do, isn't it?' He hoped to God he wasn't leading her on.

She pursed her lips and then straightened with a nod. 'I've shared things with you I've never told another living soul.'

It made him feel privileged, honoured. It made him feel insanely suffocated too.

Lines of strain fanned around her mouth. He'd caused those. He took her arm, his chest burning. 'It must be time for that cake.' Cake would buck her up. She'd eventually realise that this— that friendship—would be for the best.

They found a funky bustling café on the main street and ordered tea and cake. When the waitress brought their order over, Marianna glanced at Ryan from beneath her lashes before fiddling with her teaspoon. 'You really don't mean to visit your mother today?'

Her too casual tone had him immediately on guard. 'Why is that so hard for you to believe?'

Her shoulder lifted. 'It's just that you've flown all this way…'

He'd done what he'd come here to do. His mother was recovering. As far as he was concerned, the sooner they left now, the better.

She stirred two packets of sugar into her tea, not meeting his eye. 'You never asked me what your mother and I spoke about that first day.'

He pulled his tea towards him. 'Is it relevant to anything?'

She sent him an exasperated glare.

He sipped his tea. He tried to get comfortable on his chair. In the end he gave up. 'Fine! What did you and Stacey talk about?'

'You.'

He blinked. Not the baby?

'She told me the biggest regret of her life was leaving you with your grandmother.'

A ball of lead settled in the pit of Ryan's stomach. He moistened suddenly dry lips. He'd been doing everything he could to avoid being alone with his mother. He set his mug down with more force than necessary. 'No doubt she was just making excuses.'

'Oh, it wasn't anything like that.'

He suddenly frowned. 'If she made you feel uncomfortable, I'm very sorry.'

Her head shot up. 'It was nothing like that!'

A breath eased out of him. Good.

'I mean, I'm sure your mother likes me and everything, but, frankly, I doubt what I think of her matters to her one jot.'

He raised his hands, at a loss. 'So...'

'It was my opinion of you that mattered to her. She wanted to defend those...lone-wolf tendencies of yours.'

She'd what!

'And your opinion—what you think of her—that's what really mattered to her.'

He stared at her, unable to utter a word. If what Marianna said was true, and she had no reason to lie, then…then that meant Stacey cared for him. *That* was what Marianna was saying, whether she realised it or not. His breath jammed in his chest. On one level he knew Stacey must, but it had never been the kind of caring he'd been able to rely on, to trust in or to give himself over to.

For pity's sake, he didn't need the same family ties that Marianna did! He'd spent a lifetime guarding his privacy, his…isolation. He sat back. 'You want me to go and see her, don't you?' He glared. 'You want me to give her the opportunity to tell me what she told you?'

Marianna seemed impervious to his glare. She forked a piece of cake into her mouth and shrugged. 'What would it hurt?' she finally said.

What would it hurt? It'd… He suddenly frowned. What would it hurt?

'You want to bring our child to Australia to visit, yes?'

'Yes.'

'You'll be introducing our child to Stacey, yes?'

'Yes.'

'Don't you think the…tension between the two of you could be…awkward for our child?'

A tiny part of his heart clenched. 'You'd prefer it if I didn't let Stacey see our child?'

She huffed out a sigh and shook her head. 'No, Ryan, that's *not* what I'm saying.'

His heart started to thump, the blood thundering through his body. It hit him then that if he wanted to be the best father he could be, then making peace with his family would be necessary. He couldn't project his own issues with his mother onto his child. That would be patently unfair and potentially harmful to the child. He wanted to protect his son or daughter, help it grow up healthy in body and mind, not turn it into a neurotic mess.

Nausea surged through him. How did one go about fixing a relationship like his and Stacey's?

He glanced at the woman opposite. She'd tell him to listen to what Stacey had to say. She'd tell him to listen with an open heart. He passed a hand across his face. How did one unlock something that had been sealed shut for so long? It was a crazy idea. It—

Do it for the baby.

He stilled. If he wanted to do better than his parents had, he wouldn't run away when the going got tough. He pushed his shoulders back. It was time to man up and face his demons. It was time to lay them to rest.

'Fine.'

Marianna glanced up from her cake. 'Fine what?'

'I'll go and see Stacey.' Though, he had no idea what on earth he was going to say to her.

'You will?' she breathed.

There it was again, that look in her eye. He should never have brought her with him to Australia. *What had he been thinking?* He hadn't been thinking…at least, not with his head. He leaned towards her. 'Mari, even if I do patch up every rift between me and my family, that doesn't change things between us.'

She blinked.

He tried to choose his words carefully. 'It won't make me a family man. I'm never going to be the kind of man who can make you happy. You understand that, don't you?'

She tossed her head. 'Of course.'

His heart shrivelled to the size of a pea. He knew her too well, could see through her deceptions. She didn't believe him. She thought she could change him. She thought he'd offer her love, marriage, the works. If he didn't offer her those things would she keep his child from him?

A noose tightened about his throat, squeezing the air from his body. Marrying for the sake of their child would be a mistake—one that would destroy all of them. Anger slashed through him then. He should never have slept with her! And why couldn't she have kept her word? She'd sworn, *No promises!*

He shot to his feet. 'I'm going.'

'What, now?'

She started to rise too, but he shook his head. 'Stay and finish your cake.' He didn't give her time to reply, but turned on his heel and strode away.

Ryan tapped on the door to his mother's room, surprised to find her alone.

'You just missed Rebecca and Lulu,' she told him.

A stuffed cat with ludicrously long skinny legs had fallen behind the chair and he picked it up and stared at it, rather than at Stacey.

'Oh, dear.' Stacey sat up a little straighter in bed. 'You better take that home with you when you leave. It's Lulu's favourite. She'll be beside herself if she can't find Kitty Cat.'

That was why it looked familiar. He nodded. 'Right.'

'Colin should be along any minute. He promised to bring me a custard tart for afternoon tea.'

What was it with women and cake?

'Should I text and tell him to pick one up for you too?'

He shook his head and then realised he had barely said a word since walking into her room. 'No, thank you.' Eating custard tarts with his mother and her husband didn't fill him with a huge amount of enthusiasm. 'I…uh…how are you feeling?'

'Very well, thank you. The doctors are very happy with my progress.'

'That's good news.'

'The man you called in—the specialist—is a real wizard apparently. The rest of the staff have been whispering what an honour it is to see him in action.'

'Excellent.'

They glanced at each other and then quickly away again. An awkward silence descended. Ryan moved to stare out of the window.

'How is your Marianna doing?'

It wasn't so much the words as the tone that had

an imaginary rope tightening around his neck and coiling down his body, binding him with suffocating tightness. He made an impatient movement to try and dispel the sense of constriction. 'She's not *my* Marianna.' And he wasn't *her* Ryan. The sooner everyone understood that, the better.

'Oh.'

He grimaced, wondering if he'd been too forceful.

'She's a lovely young woman.'

'She is.' But how on earth had he let her talk him into coming to see Stacey like this? 'We walked around to Gran's house this morning.'

'Ah.'

Ah? What the hell was that supposed to mean?

'Marianna encouraged you to come and see me today, didn't she?'

He halted his pacing to glance around at her. 'I don't think it was such a good idea.' He started for the door. 'I don't see the point in raking over the past.'

'Sit down, Ryan.'

His mother's voice held a note of command that made him falter. He turned and folded his arms, the stupid Kitty Cat still dangling from his hand.

'Please.'

He stared at the stuffed toy. He thought about Marianna. He knew how disappointed she'd be if he left now. He didn't want to disappoint her. At least, not on that head. He sat down.

'I want to tell you what I told Marianna when I first met her.'

He pulled in a breath. 'Which was?'

'That the biggest regret of my life was leaving you with your grandmother.'

He couldn't look at her, afraid his face would betray his disbelief and bitterness.

From the corner of his eye he saw her lean towards him. 'Will you listen? I mean *really* listen?'

With an effort he unclenched his hands from around the stuffed toy. 'Sure.'

She didn't speak for a long moment, but still he refused to look at her.

'It's hard to know where to start precisely, but we may as well start with the breakdown of my marriage to your father. You see, I thought it all my fault.'

That made him glance up and he tried not to wince at her pallor or the way she pleated and unpleated the bed sheet. 'Are you're sure you're up to this? Maybe we should wait until you've been sent home with a clean bill of health.'

'No!' She gave a short laugh. 'I'm under no illusion that I'll ever get another shot at this.'

He could just walk out, but Marianna's face rose in his mind. He cast another quick glance in his mother's direction. Walking out now might cause her more distress. He forced himself to remain in his seat and nod. 'Fine.'

'Ryan, I only meant to leave you with your grandmother for a couple of weeks. I needed to find a new place to live.'

'But Andrew—' his father '—had gone. There was no need for you to move out of the house as well.'

'I couldn't afford the rent on my own.'

'He would've had to pay you child maintenance. That would've helped.'

'I...I refused it.'

His head rocked back.

'As I said, I blamed myself for our split and it didn't seem right to me at the time to take his money.'

'You thought *that* in my best interests?'

'I thought that if I could just get a job...find a cheap place to rent, that I could make things perfect for us and...' She lifted a hand and then let it drop again. 'Getting a job proved harder than I expected. Eventually I managed to find one in the kitchen of a cruise ship, but it meant being away for months on end.'

Ryan folded his arms. 'You were gone for three years!'

'I know,' she whispered. 'I'm sorry. I saved every dollar I could and came home to make a life with you and—'

He leapt up to pace the room again. 'Let's not pretty it up. You met Colin on that cruise liner, got pregnant, and came back here to start a family with him.' *With Colin not with Ryan.*

'But you were part of our plans. We wanted you to live with us. It's just…when I came back it was as if you hated me.'

'I was seven years old. I barely knew you!'

'I cried for a week.'

'Poor you.'

She flinched and he knew he should feel ashamed of himself, but all he felt was a deep, abiding anger. 'From memory I don't recall you expending a whole lot of energy in an effort to win me over.'

'You brought all of my hidden insecurities to the surface,' she whispered. 'I told myself I deserved your anger and resentment. I didn't want to wreck things with Colin…and I had a new baby. I had to consider them. You were happy with your grandmother. It seemed best to leave you with her for a bit longer.'

A bit longer, though, had become forever.

He spun around and glared. 'Never once did you put my needs first.'

She paled. 'I didn't mean it to happen that way. I was crippled by guilt, a lack of confidence and low self-esteem. I never realised, though, that you would be the one to pay the price for those things.'

His lips twisted. In other words things had got tough and she hadn't been able to deal with them. But something in her face caught at him, tugged at some part of him that still wanted to believe in her.

Idiot!

He tried to smother the confusion that converged on him with anger.

'You're never going to forgive me, are you?'

'It's not about forgiveness.' His voice sounded cold even to his own ears. 'It's about trust. I don't trust you to ever put me and mine first. I don't trust you to ever have my back.'

She pressed both hands to her chest, her eyes filling. 'Heavens, your father and I really did a job on you, didn't we?'

'You taught me at a very young age how the world works. It's a lesson I haven't forgotten.'

'Son, please...'

He resented her use of the word.

'Tell me that you at least trust Marianna, that you don't keep her at arm's length.'

He gave a harsh bark of laughter. He wanted to trust Marianna. He couldn't deny it, but nor could he trust the impulse. An ache rose up through him—an ache for all of those things he could never have, all of those things Marianna wanted from him that he was unable to give. *Impossible!* The best way to deal with such delusions, the smartest, most logical course of action, was to deliver them a swift mortal blow.

He whirled back to Stacey. 'Trust? What you taught me, *Mother*, was the frailties and weaknesses of women. I'm ready for that. When motherhood and the responsibility of raising a child become too much for Marianna, I'll be there for my child. *I* won't abandon it.'

A gasp in the doorway had him spinning around. Marianna stood there pale and shaking, her eyes dark and bruised. Without another word, she turned on her heel and spun away.

CHAPTER ELEVEN

THE EXPRESSION IN Marianna's eyes pushed all thought from Ryan's mind. He surged forward and caught her wrist, bringing her to a halt. 'Wait, Mari—'

She swung back, her eyes savage. 'Don't call me that!'

He swallowed back a howl. 'You have to let me explain.'

'Explain? No explanation is necessary! You made yourself perfectly clear, and I have to say it was most enlightening to find what you really think of me and our current situation.'

It hit him then how badly he'd hurt her and it felt as if he'd thrust a knife deep into his own heart. He let her go and staggered back a step, wondering what on earth was happening to him, searching his mind for a way to make things right—to stop her from looking at him as if he were a monster.

'To think I thought… And all this time you've been thinking I would *abandon* our child?'

The jagged edges of her laugh sliced into him. Marianna might be impulsive, passionate and headstrong, but she was also full of love and loyalty. He need look no further than her relationships with her brothers for proof of that. The truth that had been growing inside him, the truth he'd been hiding from, slammed into him now, bowing his shoulders and making him fall back a step. She would never abandon her child. *Never.*

What right did he have to thrust his worst-case scenario onto her? How could he have been so stupid? So…*blind*?

His chest cramped. He'd held on to that mistaken belief as an excuse to justify remaining close to her. Because he'd wanted to be close to her.

She reached out and stabbed a finger to his chest. 'Stay away from me,' she rasped, her eyes bright with unshed tears. 'I will let you know when the baby is born, but you can't ask anything else of me.'

She wheeled away from him, making for the door. *He couldn't let her go!* He started after her, not sure what he could say but unable to bear losing sight of her. Rebecca, holding Lulu, stepped in front of him, bringing him up short. He couldn't thrust her aside, not when she was holding the baby. He made to go around her, but she laid a hand on his chest. 'You can't go after her when you look like that. You can't go after her without a plan.'

He lurched over to the chair and fell into it. A plan? He'd need a miracle!

'So it's true.' His mother's words broke into the darkness surrounding him. 'You're in love with her.'

He lifted his head and looked at her. In love with Marianna? Yes. The knowledge should surprise him more than it did. 'What do I do?' The words broke from him.

She didn't flinch from his gaze. 'We play to your strengths.' He could hardly believe she was still talking to him after all he'd just flung at her.

'You're a logical man. What does Marianna want?'

'Passion, an undying love, to never be bored.' The words left him without hesitation.

'Can you give her those things?'

He recalled the way her brothers had taunted him with their stupid Paulo joke. The fact, though, was there was a thread of truth running beneath that. What if, a month down the track, Marianna dumped him?

Darkness speared into him. For a moment it hurt to even breathe.

No! He shoved his shoulders back. He wouldn't give her the opportunity to get bored. He wouldn't let their life and relationship become dull. He loved her—heart and soul—and if she'd just give him the chance he'd give her all the passion and intensity that her generous heart yearned for. He set his mouth—he'd make it his life's work.

He met his mother's gaze. 'I can give her those things.'

'You'll need to give a hundred per cent of yourself. Everything,' she warned.

Fine.

'I'm talking about your *time* here, Ryan.'

He frowned—what was she talking about?

'You're going to need to focus all your efforts on Marianna if you want to win her back.'

It hit him then—the Conti contract! If he signed on the dotted line, they'd need him on board from the week after next. He'd be working sixty-hour weeks for at least a month.

He swore. He scratched a hand through his hair. If he managed to smooth things over in the coming week with Marianna, maybe she'd let him off the hook for the following month and—

Fat chance! She'd demand all of him. Damn it! Why did she have to be so demanding? Why so unreasonable?

Suck it up, buddy. After the way you just acted, Marianna deserves to have any demand met, deserves proof of your sincerity.

Acid burned his throat. Panic rolled through him. What if he didn't succeed in smoothing things over?

What if she never forgave him?

He shot to his feet, paced the length of the room before flinging himself back into the chair. If she never forgave him he'd have lost both her and the Conti contract. Where was the sense in that?

He couldn't throw away all of that hard work. He couldn't just dismiss months' worth of nail-biting preparation. This was the contract that would set him up long term, would guarantee his livelihood for the rest of his working life and cement him as one of the business's leading lights. The Conti contract would prove once and for all that his grandmother's faith in him had been justified! He *couldn't* walk away.

Darkness descended over him, swallowing him whole. A moment later a single light pierced the darkness, making him lift his head. But what if he did win Marianna's forgiveness? What if she did agree to marry him, build a family with him…to love him? A yearning stronger than anything he'd ever experienced gripped him now. Wasn't winning Marianna's love worth any risk?

His heart pounded so hard he thought he'd crack a rib. No contract meant anything without Marianna and his child by his side. The knowledge filtered through him, scaring him senseless, but he refused to turn away from it. There'd be no point to any of his success—small or large—if he couldn't share it with Marianna and their child. He lifted his head. 'For Marianna, I'll make the time.'

Marianna stumbled into her cottage, clicking on all the lights in an attempt to push back the darkness, but it didn't work—not when the darkness was inside her. Forty hours of travel clung to her like a haze of grit. All she wanted to do was shower and fall into bed. The exhaustion, though, was worth not having had to clap eyes on Ryan again.

She halted in the doorway to her bedroom—the bed unmade, the sheets dishevelled from her and Ryan's lovemaking.

She dropped her bags and with a growl she pulled the sheets from the bed, resisting the urge to bury her face in them to see if they still carried a trace of Ryan's scent. She dumped them straight into the washing machine, set it going and then, leaving her clothes where they fell, she pushed herself under the stinging hot spray of the shower, doing what she could to rub the effects of travel and heartbreak from her body. She succeeded with the former, but it gave her little comfort.

Like a robot she dressed, remade the bed and forced herself to eat scrambled eggs. She didn't think she'd ever feel hungry again, but she had to keep eating for the baby's sake.

In the next moment she shot to her feet, the utter tidiness of the room setting her teeth on edge. With a growl, she pushed over the stack of magazines on the coffee table so they fell in an untidy sprawl. She messed up the cushions on the sofa, threw a dishtowel across the back of a dining chair—haphazardly. She didn't push her chair in at the table, and she slammed her plate and cutlery on the sink, but didn't wash them. She shoved the tea, coffee and sugar canisters on the kitchen bench out of perfect alignment.

None of it made her feel any better.

A tap on the door accompanied with a 'Marianna?' pulled her up short.

Nico. She swallowed. 'Come on through,' she called out.

He sauntered into the room. 'I saw the lights on and thought you must be home. You should've let us know to expect you. I'd have collected you from the airport.'

He pulled up short and took her in at a single glance. He'd always managed to do that, but she lifted her chin. She didn't want to talk about it.

'Alone?' he finally ventured.

She moved to fill the kettle. 'Yes.'

He was silent for a moment. 'How's Ryan's mother?'

'Out of danger and recovering beautifully.' She'd ring Stacey tomorrow to double-check that the scene in her hospital room hadn't had any detrimental effects on her recovery. And to assure her that she wouldn't prevent any of them from seeing the baby once it was born.

'That's good news.'

'It is.'

He paused again. 'How are you?'

She met his gaze and his expression gentled. 'Oh, Mari.'

She couldn't keep it together then. She walked into his arms and burst into tears, her heart shredding afresh with every sob. *Why couldn't Ryan love her?*

She refused to let the words fall from her lips, though, and she did what she could to pull herself together. She moved away, scrubbing the tears from her cheeks. 'I'm sorry. I'm tired.'

'You have nothing to apologise for.'

Was that true?

'I take it we shouldn't expect Ryan any time soon?'

Her brother deserved some form of explanation. 'I told him I'd let him know when the baby was born.'

Nico's eyes darkened in concern.

'It's okay.' She could see he didn't believe her and she didn't blame him. It wasn't okay, but there was nothing she could do about it. She just had to get on with it the best she could. 'We…we just messed up, that's all. And I find that I can't be… friends with him.'

He swore softly in Italian.

She managed a smile. 'It's okay, Nico. I'm a big girl. I will never denigrate him to my child. When we meet I will be polite and calm. That's what will be best for my darling *topolino*.'

He took her hand. 'But what's best for you?'

She could never tell him and Angelo all that had passed between her and Ryan. They'd have to find a way to be polite to him too. She didn't want to make that more difficult for them than it had to be. 'The baby has to come first. That's what matters to me.'

He swore again and his grip on her hand tightened. 'He's broken your heart!'

She moistened her lips and dredged up another smile. 'Some would say it's no less than I deserve for that trail of Paulos I've left in my wake.'

'I wouldn't agree.'

'I know that,' she whispered back, managing a genuine smile this time. Ryan might be a complete and utter idiot, but he had eased her fears about her brothers.

Time to change the subject. 'Where's Angelo?'

'Out with Kayla.'

'Naturally.'

They grinned at each other. 'We've missed you, Mari.'

She gave him a quick hug. 'I've missed you too.'

She made tea and they settled on the sofa. 'Now catch me up on all the news.'

Ryan turned the hire car in at the gates of Vigneto Calanetti and made his way down the long drive.

He'd been away less than three weeks, but he swore the grapevines were lusher and greener. The sky was blue and the day was warm, and inside his chest his heart pounded like a jackhammer.

Would she see him?

Please, God, let her spare him ten minutes. Please give him at least ten minutes to make his mark, to try and win her love.

He parked the hire car out at the front of Nico's villa. He wanted to race straight across to Marianna's cottage, but instinct warned him to check in with her brothers first. He wanted to do things right—by the book. He didn't want to make things worse for Marianna than he already had.

He recalled the last look she'd sent him, filled with pain and utter betrayal, and his gut clenched. *Please, God, let her be okay. Please let her and the baby be in good health.*

He knocked on the villa's wide-open door and tried to control the pounding of his heart. If Marianna should appear now...

He stared down the hallway, willing it to happen. A figure did appear. A male figure. It was what he'd expected, but he had to lock his knees against the disappointment. 'Nico,' he said in greeting as the other man strode down the hallway.

'Ryan.'

They stared at each other for a long moment. Nico bit back a sigh. 'She's not going to want to see you.'

'I can't say as though I blame her. I messed up.' Ryan pulled in a breath. 'I messed up badly. I won't retaliate if you want to take a swing at me.' He wouldn't even block the blow.

'I'm not going to hit you, but…whatever it is you want to say, can't you put it in an email?'

He moistened suddenly dry lips. 'I want to ask her to marry me.'

'For the sake of the baby?'

He shook his head. 'Not for the baby.'

'I see.'

Ryan suspected he did.

'I suppose I better take you to her.'

Ryan followed him through the house, out the French doors and across the terrace towards the outbuildings. 'You think I need an escort? I have no intention of harming a single hair on Mari's head.'

'I realise that, but my loyalty lies with my sister.' He cast a sidelong glance at Ryan. 'My one consolation is that you look in even worse shape than she does.'

Ryan seized Nico by the shoulders and dragged

him to a halt, fear cramping his chest. 'She isn't well?' he croaked.

'Physically she's fine. She's taking very good care of her health.'

He released Nico, dragged a hand down his face and then continued to plant one foot in front of the other, his blood pounding a furious tempo through his body. 'That's…that's something.'

'It is.'

They walked through the shadowed cool of the vineyard's cellar door, skirting a group of tourists wine tasting, and out the back to where the great barrels of wine were stored, and then beyond that to the fermentation vats. That was when he saw her. He pulled up short and drank her in like a starving man.

In the soft light her hair fizzed about her face. He watched her direct a team of three workers to move barrels from one location to another and she then checked the gauges on the nearest vat. Her slim, vigorous form so familiar to him it made his arms ache with the need to hold her.

And then she turned and saw him. She froze. Her every muscle tightened and a bitter taste rose in his mouth. He did that to her. He made her tense and unhappy.

He thought she'd simply turn around and walk away. After several fraught moments, however, she lifted her chin and moved towards them. But her body that had once moved with such freedom and grace was now held tight and rigid. He had to bite back a protest. *How could he have done that to her?*

'I don't want you here, Ryan. Please go.'

Her pallor and the dark circles beneath her eyes beat at him. 'I can't say that I blame you.' He stared down at his hands and then back at her. 'I came to apologise. What I said—'

'Pah!' She slashed a hand through the air.

He tried to take her hand, but she snapped back a step, her eyes flashing.

He swallowed and nodded. 'What I said…I was wrong. I know you will love our child with your whole heart. I know you will never abandon it. And just because that's what I experienced in my family…' He shook his head. 'I had no right tarring you with the same brush. It was an excuse I was hiding behind. It let me justify to myself the amount of time I was spending with you. It helped me keep my distance. I…I didn't realise I'd been lying to myself, though, until you walked out of Mum's hospital room.'

She folded her arms and glanced away, tapped a foot. 'How is your mother?'

'Excellent. She sends her love. So does Rebecca.'

She finally glanced back. 'I accept your apology, Ryan, but I'm afraid you and I are never going to be friends.'

'I don't want to be friends.'

She paled and eased back another step. 'I'm glad we have that sorted.' Spinning on her heel, she stalked away.

'Damn it, Marianna!' Had she wilfully mis-understood him? 'I want a whole lot more than friendship,' he hollered to her back. 'I want it all—love, marriage, babies…a family.' He punctuated each word with a stab in the air, but she didn't turn around. *'With you!'*

She didn't so much as falter. He shook off Nico's restraining hand and set off after her, muttering a curse under his breath. He waited, though, until she'd reached her stone cottage before catching her up.

She wheeled on him. 'Get out of my house!'

'I'll leave once you hear me out.'

'I've heard enough!'

'You've only heard what you want to hear!'

'Mari?' Nico stood in the doorway, one eyebrow raised.

Ryan planted his feet all the more solidly. No one was kicking him off the premises until he'd done what he'd come here to do.

Marianna's eyes flashed as if she'd read that intention in his face. She glanced at her watch. 'If his car is still here in ten minutes, come back with Angelo.'

With a nod, Nico left.

She was going to give him ten minutes?

He couldn't speak for a moment. He had to fight the urge to haul her into his arms and kiss her. If he did any such thing he'd deserve to be thrown out.

She remained where she stood, bathed in the sunlight that poured in at the kitchen windows, tapping her foot. She glanced at her watch as if counting down every second of his allotted ten minutes.

He missed her smile and her teasing. He even missed her untidiness and her temper. He'd rather she threw something at him than this *nothingness*.

'Since you left,' he started, 'I've been in a misery of guilt, a misery of mortification at my stupidity, and a misery of loss.'

'Good.' She lifted her chin. 'Why should you be

exempt? I've been miserable on my baby's behalf that its father is such a jerk.'

His head throbbed. What was he doing here other than making a fool of himself? He should turn around and leave. She loathed him and he couldn't blame her. She was going to laugh at him; throw his love back in his face.

It's no less than you deserve.

He pulled in a breath and steeled himself. 'I love you, Mari.' He had to say what he'd come here to say.

Her eyes narrowed. 'I told you not to call me that.'

He ground his teeth together, unclenched them to say, 'I love you, *Marianna*.'

She moved in to peer up into his face. 'Piffle.' She stalked past him to the dining table, but she didn't sit.

'I want to marry you.'

She turned at that and laughed. He rocked back, her expression running him through like a sword. He locked his knees. 'You think it funny?'

'Absolutely hilarious!' But her flashing eyes and fingers that curved into claws told a different story. 'You've lost whatever advantage you think you had. You believe I'm going to withhold your child from you and this is your way to try and claw back all you've lost. I'm sorry, Ryan, but it's not going to work.'

The last puff of hope eased out of him in a single breath.

'You needn't worry, though.' She tossed her hair. 'I'm not going to stop you from seeing our child, but the visitation arrangements will be on my terms.'

He moistened his lips. 'This isn't about the baby, Mari.'

She turned away with a shrug, not even bothering to correct him—as if it no longer mattered to her what he called her. She glanced at her watch.

This couldn't be it! Where would he find that strength to walk away from her?

Think! How could he win her heart? *What is it she wants?*

He pulled up short. Passion, an undying love, and to never be bored—those were the things Marianna wanted. *Could* he give them to her?

He pulled in a breath and channelled his inner thespian. 'You want to know what I've been doing for the last two weeks?' He roared the words and she started and turned around, her eyes wide.

He stalked over to where she stood and stabbed

a finger at her. 'I've been working on my relation-ships with my family so I'd have something of worth to offer you! And you want to laugh in my face and act as if it's nothing when it's been one of the most difficult and…and frightening things I've ever done?'

She moistened her lips and edged away. 'I didn't intend to belittle your…um, efforts. I'm…I'm sure they've been very admirable.'

'My efforts!' He threw both hands in the air and then paced the length of the room. He prayed to God he wasn't frightening her. He hated yelling at her, but if that was what she needed as proof of his love, then he'd do it.

He swung back to find her biting her thumbnail and staring at him, a frown in her eyes.

'If I'm correct it's not my efforts being dispar-aged but my intentions!'

He glared at her as hard as he could. She pulled her hand away from her mouth and straightened. 'You come in here and say outlandish things and expect me to believe you?'

'Saying *I love you* is not outlandish!' How could he make her see that? His gaze landed on the vase her brothers had given her. He grabbed it and lifted it above his head. 'I can't live without you, Mari! How can I get that through your thick skull?'

Marianna's bottom lip started to wobble, though she did her best to stop it. 'You're…you're going to throw a vase at me?'

He stared at her, and then rolled his shoulder. 'Of course not.' He lowered the vase, grimaced. 'I was going to throw it on the floor as evidence of my…high emotion.'

She couldn't drag her gaze from him. It hurt her to look at him, but she had a feeling it'd hurt more to look away.

I can't live without you!

She swallowed. 'Please don't break the vase. I… it has sentimental value.' Whenever she looked at it, it reminded her of her and Ryan's dinner with her brothers here in this cottage, and the conversation she and Ryan had had afterwards…how kind he'd been…and gentle.

She much preferred that Ryan to the shouting, angry man who'd just raged at her. It occurred to her now that his calm and his control had given her a safe harbour—that was what she wanted, not a stormy sea.

Ryan set the vase back on the table just as her

brothers burst into the room—their bodies tense, fists clenched and eyes blazing. Had they heard him yelling at her?

Angelo seemed to grow in size. 'Nobody speaks to our sister like that!'

They moved towards Ryan with unmistakable intent. 'No!' she screeched. Ryan's time might be up, but... She did the only thing she could think of. She ran across the room and hurled herself into Ryan's arms. He caught her easily, as if she weighed nothing. He held her as if she were precious.

Her heart pounded and it was all she could do not to melt against him. 'Turn me around,' she murmured in his car.

He turned so that she could face her brothers. They glared at her, hands on hips. 'Go away,' she ordered.

They didn't move.

She tightened her hold on Ryan's neck, loving the feel of all his hardness and strength pressed against her. 'I have things under control here.'

Nico raised an eyebrow. Angelo snorted.

She widened her eyes, made them big and pleading. 'Please?' she whispered.

Muttering, they left.

Two beats passed. Marianna swallowed. 'You can put me down now.'

'Do I have to?'

'Yes.'

The minute he set her feet back on the ground, she moved away from him—put the table between them. The flare of his nostrils told her that her caution hurt him. She didn't want to hurt him. She loved him with every fibre of her being, but she couldn't accept anything less than his whole heart in return.

The silence stretched, pulling her nerves taut. She wiped damp palms down her trousers. 'You have to understand that I find your declaration a little unbelievable.'

'Why?'

'Lone wolf,' she whispered.

He adjusted his stance. 'That was a lie I told myself to make me feel better. It doesn't matter what happens today, I'm never going to be a lone wolf again. That all changed when I thought I'd lost you.'

He strode around the table and to her utter amazement dropped to his knees in front of her. He seized her hands and held them to his lips, and then his brow. Her heart hammered so hard she thought it'd pound a path right out of her chest.

'I'm nothing without you, Mari.'

And there it was, the thrill she couldn't suppress whenever he said her name.

'What I feel for you is so encompassing, so over-whelming it makes the thought of living without you unbearable. It's why I'd been resisting it so long and why I fought against it so fiercely. But it's no use fighting it any more or hiding from the truth. Marianna, you make me want to be a bet-ter man.'

He glanced up at her and what she saw in his face pierced her to the very marrow.

'Knowing you has brought untold treasures to my life—a baby.'

She nodded. He would cherish their child.

'You've shown me the way back to my family.'

Had he really reconciled with his mother? What about his father and the rest of his siblings?

'You've given me a vision of what my life could be like.'

He hauled himself upright, kissed the tips of her fingers before releasing her hands and stepping back. 'I understand your hesitation. I understand that you might see me as a poor bet.' He glanced at his watch and his chest heaved. 'I've taken up enough of your time. I should give you the space to consider all that I've said.'

He turned to leave and it was the hunch in his shoulders, the way they drooped in utter defeat that did it—that blasted away the last of her doubts. She pressed a hand to her heart, her pulse leaping every which way. 'You really do love me.'

He swung back, hope alive in his face. She could feel her face crumple. 'But you yelled at me.'

And then she burst into tears.

Ryan swooped across and pulled her into his arms, holding her as if he never meant to let her go. 'I only yelled at you to prove that I really do love you, to prove I could give you the passion that you said you've always wanted.'

She eased back, scrubbed a hand across her face. 'I hated it! I'm an idiot forever thinking that's what I wanted.'

He swiped his thumbs across her cheeks. 'You're not an idiot.'

'I love you,' she whispered.

He nodded gravely. '*That* might make you an idiot.'

'Are you going to break my heart?'

He shook his head. 'I'm going to take the very

best care of your heart. I'm going to do everything within my power to make you happy.' The tension in his shoulders eased a fraction. 'I'm going to be very relieved if not yelling at you is on that list, though.' He smoothed his hands down the sides of her face. 'I hated yelling at you. I'm sorry it upset you.'

She wound her arms around his neck. 'Then I'm not an idiot. I'm the luckiest woman in the world.'

Her smile started up in the centre of her and reached out to every extremity. 'You really love me?' It wasn't that she didn't believe him. She just wanted to hear him say it again.

'I really love you.' His grin was all the assurance she needed.

'I really love you too,' she said, just in case he needed to hear it again as well.

'Will you marry me?'

A lump promptly lodged in her throat, momentarily robbing her of the ability to speak.

'I meant to go down on one knee and propose properly.'

She swallowed the lump. 'Don't you dare let go of me yet.'

'That's what I was hoping you'd say.'

This tough loner of a man had really trusted his

heart and happiness to her? She touched his face in wonder. He let out a ragged breath. Plastered as closely as she was to him, she could feel how tightly he held himself in check. 'That…and yes,' he rasped.

She came back to herself with a start, the uncertainty in his eyes catching at her. 'Yes.'

He blinked.

'Yes, I will marry you. Yes, I will keep your heart safe. Yes, we'll build a wonderful family together, and grow old together and be generous with our love to all who want and need it.'

'You mean that?'

She reached up on tiptoe to cup his face. 'I love you, Ryan. How could you possibly think I would want anything else?'

'Can I kiss you now?' he groaned.

'In just a moment.'

He groaned louder.

'I want you to tell me how you reconciled with your mother…and father?' He nodded at the question in her voice. 'How did that all come about? I mean, you were so angry with them.'

He lifted her in his arms and strode across to the sofa with her, settling her in his lap as if she belonged there, as if he had no intention of letting her go anywhere else for a very long time. It sent another delicious thrill racing through her. She pressed a kiss to his cheek. 'I'm not saying you weren't entitled to your anger.'

'But it was time to let it go.'

She let out a breath she hadn't realised she'd been holding.

'And I discovered that forgiveness is an act of hope.'

Her heart soared. 'Oh, Ryan, I'm so glad.'

'I'd made such a terrible mistake with you and the thought of not winning your forgiveness was a torment. The thought I might be putting my parents through a similar torment shook some sense into me.' He met her gaze. 'I couldn't live with that thought.'

Of course he couldn't. He had a heart that was too big and generous for that.

'When you left I was beside myself.'

He would've been. She could see that now.

'And they all rallied around me, so worried for me. It made me realise that they do all care for me.'

'They do.'

He touched her cheek. 'I'd have never realised if it wasn't for you.'

She ran her hands across his shoulders and down

his arms, revelling in the sculpted strength of him. 'We're good for each other, Ryan. I've heard of people finding their soul mates, I knew that kind of love existed. I knew it couldn't be wrong to hold out for it.'

'My soul mate,' he said as if testing the idea on his tongue.

'Your rationality balances out my flights of fancy.'

'Your sense of fun balances out my seriousness.'

'Your control balances out my, uh…lack of restraint.'

He ran a finger down the V made by the collar of her shirt, making her shiver. 'I promise never to yell at you again.'

'But…' She lifted one shoulder. 'What if I'm testing your patience beyond endurance, being stubborn and headstrong?'

He pressed a kiss to the tender spot behind her ear. 'I'll find a different way to get your attention.'

She arched against him. 'Mmm, I like the sound of that. I promise never to throw another vase at you.'

He eased back, a smile in his eyes. 'I don't know. That kind of thing keeps a man on his toes.' His eyes darkened. 'Mind you, I'll be doing my very best to not provoke you into throwing vases.'

'Ryan?'

'Yes?'

'You can kiss me now.'

His grin became teasing, wolfish, and a thrill shot through her. His mouth descended towards hers. He stopped millimetres short. 'Do you have to go back to work this afternoon?'

Her breath hitched. 'Not unless I want to.'

'You're really not going to want to,' he promised.

She tilted her chin, a smile building in the depths of her. 'Prove it.'

So he did.

* * * * *

MILLS & BOON®
Large Print – January 2016

The Greek Commands His Mistress
Lynne Graham

A Pawn in the Playboy's Game
Cathy Williams

Bound to the Warrior King
Maisey Yates

Her Nine Month Confession
Kim Lawrence

Traded to the Desert Sheikh
Caitlin Crews

A Bride Worth Millions
Chantelle Shaw

Vows of Revenge
Dani Collins

Reunited by a Baby Secret
Michelle Douglas

A Wedding for the Greek Tycoon
Rebecca Winters

Beauty & Her Billionaire Boss
Barbara Wallace

Newborn on Her Doorstep
Ellie Darkins

MILLS & BOON®
Large Print – February 2016

Claimed for Makarov's Baby
Sharon Kendrick

An Heir Fit for a King
Abby Green

The Wedding Night Debt
Cathy Williams

Seducing His Enemy's Daughter
Annie West

Reunited for the Billionaire's Legacy
Jennifer Hayward

Hidden in the Sheikh's Harem
Michelle Conder

Resisting the Sicilian Playboy
Amanda Cinelli

Soldier, Hero...Husband?
Cara Colter

Falling for Mr December
Kate Hardy

The Baby Who Saved Christmas
Alison Roberts

A Proposal Worth Millions
Sophie Pembroke

MILLS & BOON®

Why shop at millsandboon.co.uk?

Each year, thousands of romance readers find their perfect read at millsandboon.co.uk. That's because we're passionate about bringing you the very best romantic fiction. Here are some of the advantages of shopping at www.millsandboon.co.uk:

* **Get new books first**—you'll be able to buy your favourite books one month before they hit the shops

* **Get exclusive discounts**—you'll also be able to buy our specially created monthly collections, with up to 50% off the RRP

* **Find your favourite authors**—latest news, interviews and new releases for all your favourite authors and series on our website, plus ideas for what to try next

* **Join in**—once you've bought your favourite books, don't forget to register with us to rate, review and join in the discussions

Visit **www.millsandboon.co.uk**
for all this and more today!